CONFLICT OF HEARTS

Somerset, at the end of World War I: Daniel Holley, unhappily married to an ailing wife and father of four grown-up children, is attracted to beautiful schoolteacher Harriet Bray, but he knows his love is hopeless. Daniel's only daughter, Amy, who dreams of becoming a milliner and is caught up in her love for young bank clerk John Tottle, looks on as the drama of Daniel and Harriet's fate and happiness gradually unfolds.

Books by Gillian Kaye
in the Linford Romance Library:

WAITING FOR MATT
HEARTBREAK AT HAVERSHAM

GILLIAN KAYE

CONFLICT OF HEARTS

Complete and Unabridged

LINFORD
Leicester

First published in Great Britain

First Linford Edition
published 1999

British Library CIP Data

Kaye, Gillian
    Conflict of hearts.—Large print ed.—
Linford romance library
1. Love stories
2. Large type books
I. Title
823.9′14 [F]

ISBN 0–7089–5486–3

Published by
F. A. Thorpe (Publishing) Ltd.
Anstey, Leicestershire

Set by Words & Graphics Ltd.
Anstey, Leicestershire
Printed and bound in Great Britain by
T. J. International Ltd., Padstow, Cornwall

This book is printed on acid-free paper

1

Amy looked at the clock above the jars of sweets and the colourful advertisements for tobacco. It said four o'clock and that meant it was nearly time to start looking for Miss Bray. Amy looked forward to this same hour every weekday afternoon — the rush of children coming in on their way home from school to spend their pennies on sweets or chocolate would be over and from where she stood behind the counter, she could see the people walking down Eastfield, passing the sweetshop affectionately known as Bartletts.

It was 1918 and first thing in the morning, the men passing on their bicycles on their way to the munitions factory were old men. The young and able were at the Front. They had been fighting and giving their lives for four long years and still the war dragged on. Then the street got busy as mothers took their children to school and did their shopping on the way home.

But punctually at four o'clock, for one brief moment, Amy was lifted out of the narrow confines of her world as Miss Bray went past, walking steadily and looking straight ahead. Harriet Bray was a teacher at St Matthew's School, tall and slim but giving no hint of frailty in her slender frame. Harriet was all the things that Amy felt that she herself was not with her five feet of restless energy capped by her turbulent red hair.

Amy's watchfulness for Miss Bray was rudely interrupted by the sound of raised voices coming from the room behind the shop. She frowned and flicked her hair back in a gesture of annoyance even though the sound was a familiar one. Her mother and father were quarrelling again.

The pattern was always the same, the high tones from Dorrie, her mother, whose once soft voice had become a never-ending complaining whine. Then her father, Daniel Holley, would speak, at first firmly then gradually losing his temper until Amy knew that she would hear the last exasperated shout as he opened the door and came into the shop.

It had happened so many times before and today was to be no exception, Amy thought resignedly. But even as she listened to the raised voices, Harriet Bray came into view and Amy's keen gaze saw the hesitation in the step then, like a miracle, the beautiful face appeared in the doorway. At the same time, to Amy's horror, the door to the back room also opened and Daniel stormed through, slamming it behind him.

He could not rush out as he usually did. Harriet stood there, calm, poised, her long brown coat fitting her neatly and smartly, her hat attractively framing her abundant brown hair.

Daniel stopped. He was a tall man,

almost forty years of age but his face was unlined and he looked so much younger. His vivid dark eyes were blazing after the quarrel and his mouth was set tight.

Amy was faltering as she looked from one to the other. She started to say something but she halted as she realised that her father and Harriet Bray were looking at each other as though no-one else in the world existed. Harriet's soft, intelligent brown eyes met the still angry ones. Her expression was serious but there was a half-smile on her lips as she gazed into his eyes.

In the end, Daniel was the first to speak.

'Amy, are you going to introduce me to your friend?' Daniel said very quietly.

Amy looked dubiously at Harriet Bray. She had spoken to her no more than a half dozen times in the past and the brief exchanges of words had always taken place in the shop. She could hardly introduce Harriet as a friend, but Harriet had lost her serious look and the smile that met Amy's was one of encouraging shyness.

'This is Miss Bray, Dad,' Amy said, her voice full of hesitation. 'She is a teacher at St Matthew's School. Miss Bray, this is my father, Daniel Holley.'

A slim, well-shaped hand was placed into Daniel's, the clasp firm.

'I am very pleased to meet you, Miss Bray. I believe I know your father. Now if you will excuse me I have some business to see to in the town.'

Harriet stood to one side and the tall figure of Daniel Holley strode out of the shop leaving Amy nervous and apprehensive. But she need not have worried. If something momentous had just happened in Harriet Bray's life, she was not going to show it. She just smiled at Amy and stepped up to the counter.

'Hello, Amy. We have my sister and her children coming to see us and I think I will take them a few sweets.

What would you suggest?'

They agreed on some raspberry pips and some alphabet comfits and Amy weighed them out then gave the bags to Harriet, said goodbye, and sighed as the graceful figure of the young teacher left the shop. Knowing that it would be quiet for a while until the men left the factories, Amy's thoughts began to wander.

Amy Holley was just eighteen years old and had spent the war years reluctantly helping her father in one of the sweet shops he owned in the Somerset town of Waterbridge. She had wanted to be a munitions worker but her father would not agree. Daniel Holley was a man of business in the small town. He owned the sweet factory and several shops and supplied the town and the stores in the surrounding villages with confectionery.

He also owned several houses and was a familiar and distinguished figure in the town riding around in his pony and trap to collect his rents. He was popular, was a good landlord and a good father.

He had married Dorrie when he had first arrived in Waterbridge from London and they had four children of whom Amy was the only girl. After the birth of their youngest child, Edmund, Dorrie had become depressed and unwell and although Daniel loved his children, he sometimes showed little patience with illness. As Amy grew up, she sensed rather than understood the unhappy relationship growing between her mother and father.

The family lived in a big house in Rhodes Place, not far from the main shopping street and opposite St Matthew's Church and Daniel had found a local woman to help Dorrie. Without Mrs Chidgey, the children's lives would have been miserable for she became the never-ending source of love that their own mother did not seem to be able to give them.

At the outbreak of war, Dorrie's mother, who lived above the sweet shop in Eastfield, became crippled with rheumatism and Dorrie moved into the shop to look after her, easing some of the tensions at Rhodes Place.

Now, with the war in its fourth year, some of those tensions from home had spilled over into the shop and the scene that Amy had just heard between her mother and father seemed to have become part of everyday life. Amy sighed. She wished that her father had more patience and that her mother would try a little harder to understand him; she wished that the war was over and last of all, something she had wished for as long as she could remember — that she was a little taller, more like Miss Bray!

Conscious as always of her lack of inches, Amy dragged out the wooden stool from under the counter, stood on it and replaced the jars she had taken from the top shelf. She did not hear the click of the shop door and almost fell off the stool in fright when she felt her waist grabbed from behind.

'Got you, Amy!' a gleeful voice said.

'Percy Venn.'

Amy jumped down from the stool and faced her assailant across the counter.

'How dare you creep up on me like that and why aren't you in your own shop?'

Her words sounded cross but her tone matched the friendly grin of the fair-haired young man who was looking cheerfully and cheekily at her. Percy and Amy had known one another from childhood, Percy being the son of Mr Venn who owned the furniture shop across the road. Percy, too, helped his father and he and Amy were good friends.

'Guess what, Amy? My call-up has come.'

His tone was jubilant but jubilation was not what Amy felt.

'Oh, Percy,' she cried, 'I thought you wouldn't have to go. The war must soon be over, surely.'

'Not go, when I've been waiting all

these months trying to convince them that I was old enough?'

Amy had seen too many young men go from the town, to join the fighting and not come back. She fought back the tears and found her hands grasped across the counter.

'Cheer up, Amy. I'll be back. Now what shall we do on my last night? Shall we go to the Palace?'

It was one of the favourite pastimes of the young people of Waterbridge to visit the Palace Theatre in the evenings. Sometimes there would be a film, often a concert party or a play. But on this occasion, Amy shook her head.

'No, I think I'd rather go for a walk. It's a nice, fine evening, isn't it?'

'Yes, it is. I'll call for you at about seven o'clock. Will that be all right?'

'Yes, it will give me plenty of time to lock up here and to have some tea.'

Amy smiled at Percy as he hurried out of the door. She was very fond of him and he was almost like another brother. He was always cheerful and had been a good companion in these gloomy times. She would miss him.

Amy's grandmother, Mrs Bartlett, and Dorrie lived above the shop and each day when Amy had put the closed notice on the shop door, she slipped upstairs to visit them and give them the day's news. Amy was Mrs Bartlett's favourite grandchild and was sympathetic when she heard the news of Percy's call-up.

Amy stayed chatting for a little while but she was tired and hungry and was glad when the time came to slip home to Rhodes Place. She made her way straight to the large kitchen at the back of the house. It was the room she loved best and she knew she would find Mrs Chidgey there.

'Hello, Mrs Chidgey,' Amy said as she entered the kitchen.

'Miss Amy, you gave me a fright.'

As the older woman turned round, Amy felt enveloped in the love and care which flowed from her. At sixty, Mrs Chidgey worked tirelessly for the family she had come to love.

Over some tea, Amy told Mrs Chidgey the news of Percy then she made her way up to her bedroom. Amy would not have admitted to vanity. She had been brought up amongst boys and considered herself as good as they were but she loved clothes and she was always poring over fashion books and making something new. Her diminutive figure did not stop her from becoming one of the smartest young ladies in the town.

She tried on what she thought of as her best dress and looked at herself in the long mirror. Satisfied with her appearance, she went downstairs where she knew she would find her brothers. The youngest of the family, Edmund, was still at school, Frank worked as a clerk in the town council offices while George, the eldest, was away at sea.

Percy, that evening, was unusually silent and it was not until they were walking along the riverbank that he began to reveal his thoughts to Amy.

'Amy,' he started to say.

She turned to look at him, wondering what was on his mind. She was used to ceaseless chatter from him and guessed that the thought of going off to the war had forced him to take a deeper look into life than he usually did. She asked her question tentatively.

'Are you worrying about going to the war, Percy?' she asked him.

'No, it's not that I worry about going. But I suppose it's made me think about the future more.'

'The future?'

'Yes, when I come back. We'll be older, different, you and I, but we've been good pals ever since I can remember.'

He stopped and turned to face her.

'If I hadn't been going away, we would have gone on, wouldn't we? Dances, walks, the Palace, having a good time. Now all that's changed and what I want to ask you, Amy, is, will

13

you get engaged to me before I go?'

She looked up at him unable to believe that he was serious. But his intention was written firmly on his face. She was silent, thinking.

'Amy, did you hear what I said?'

'Yes, I did hear, Percy, but I can't believe you really mean it. Engagement means marriage and that means love. I'm sorry, Percy, but I've never thought of you like that. It's like you said, we've been good pals. When I get engaged it will be because I love someone enough to marry them. Oh, Percy, I don't want to hurt you, not tonight. I'm very fond of you but that's not love, is it?'

The sentence ended in a question and as he looked at her serious, troubled face, he took her hand.

'It's the same for me, Amy, and I'm not sure whether it's love or not. But I do know that I'd like to go away knowing that you'll be waiting for me when I come back.'

'Percy, I don't know what to say.

I can't say what I don't feel. Please understand that I shall still be here when you come back but I don't want to get engaged. We're too young to tie ourselves down like that. When you're away, you want to be free to take a girl to a dance if you want to. I might meet someone else. I'm not saying I will but I don't want to be tied, not when I'm only eighteen.'

Amy put her hands to her face as tears came streaming down her cheeks.

'I'm sorry, Percy. I wanted this to be a happy last evening for you and now I've spoiled it.'

His arm came round her shoulders and he pulled her close to him.

'Amy Holley, you are a wonderful girl. You are so open and honest. You don't hide anything. But there's one thing you can't refuse me tonight, Amy.'

She looked puzzled.

'A kiss, Amy?' he asked quietly.

'Oh, Percy.'

She smiled and offered him her cheek.

'No, Amy.'

He turned her head towards him and gently and clumsily claimed her lips in a kiss, the first they had exchanged. As the embrace finished, Percy was smiling at her.

'That was as good as a ring on your finger and not so expensive,' he teased, and they both laughed gratefully.

Their mood lightened and they chatted happily all the way home, Percy receiving a shy kiss when they said goodbye.

In the house, Amy saw a light from under the drawing-room door and knew her father must be there. Thinking that he might like to be alone, she started to creep past but the sound of his voice halted her.

'Is that you, Amy?'

She pushed open the door and entered the room. A high ceiling set off Regency furniture to advantage and there were two glass cabinets with his collection of Worcester porcelain, which Amy loved.

'Pull up a chair and come and sit with me for a while,' he said.

Amy looked at her father. How could this be the same man who earlier in the day had been so harsh with his wife? Amy loved him so much but his impatience with her mother worried her. Even when he shouted at Dorrie, Amy felt that her sympathy was for him and she still loved him. Suddenly she felt that she wanted to tell him about Percy.

'Dad, Percy wanted us to become engaged before he went away.'

'Engaged? At your age? I hope your answer was no.'

'Well, yes, it was but I am still wondering if I should have agreed as he was going to the Front.'

Daniel put his hand on his daughter's shoulder.

'You were right to hesitate. Nothing good can come of marrying so young and you've hardly begun to live your life yet.'

'But, Dad, you and Mother were young . . . '

She stopped short thinking perhaps she had said the wrong thing. But Daniel was obviously in a confiding mood.

'Yes, I know all about that. I wasn't much more than twenty and look at me now, not yet forty with four grown-up children.'

He made a joke of it and they both laughed.

'And here you are, thinking of marriage yourself. All I can say to you, my dear, is to be absolutely certain that you love the person you marry.'

Amy was disturbed. Was he telling her that he hadn't loved Dorrie? Surely he must have done so when they first met, though now she knew that there was little love left between them. Amy felt sad and perplexed.

'But, Dad, how can you ever be sure?' she asked.

Daniel looked at the young face and sighed.

'You can't be sure, Amy, but you don't need to rush into marriage when you are so very young. Wait a while and listen to your heart. You will know, my dear, you will know.'

2

Amy was not the only young woman in Waterbridge that evening to be pondering over the perplexities of love. Harriet Bray sat in her room at the top of her home in the spacious house she shared with her mother and father in Regent Square. It was a gracious part of the town. Some of the houses still had their wrought-iron balconies and all the houses in the square had access to the trees and lawns in the gardens at its centre.

That evening, sitting in an easy chair and staring into the last red glow of the fire, Harriet reflected for a long time over the events of the day. Her mood was so intense that her thoughts ranged back over her whole life.

Her childhood, she remembered happily, had been spent in llminster. She had gone to the grammar school and then realised her ambition of becoming a teacher by going to college in London.

Her father was the head of a firm of auctioneers and estate agents and while Harriet was at college, he had moved his offices to the larger town of Waterbridge and had settled in Regent Square.

When Harriet finished college, she taught in London for a while until a vacancy occurred at Eastfield School in Waterbridge and she was delighted when she was appointed. She returned to live at home but after the freedom of her life in London was inclined to find this irksome at times. Harriet often longed for the privacy of her own lodgings. However she knew that her parents would be shocked to think that she wanted to live apart from them and she tried to settle down.

Just before the outbreak of war, when Harriet was twenty-five years old, she fell in love with a young schoolmaster who had joined the staff. They got engaged just before Richard went off to join the campaign in France, in 1914. When his death at the first battle of Ypres was announced, Harriet was broken hearted.

For months, she hardly spoke to her parents and they despaired of her ever recovering from the death of her fiancé. But as the war progressed, so many men from the town were lost and Harriet felt caught up in the web of war and shared her sorrow with those she met at school and at church.

Four years later, she was still at Eastfield, where she was much loved, still living at home with her parents and resigned to becoming a spinster schoolteacher. She loved her work and was comfortable enough at home but deep within her was the feeling that one day she must find an independent home of her own.

Harriet's greatest friend was her sister, Elizabeth, who was older than her by ten years and was married to a farmer near Taunton. She visited her parents' home regularly with her young family and Harriet was always pleased to see her nieces and nephews. Thinking of the children reminded her of the sweets she had bought for them and the innocent action which had triggered off such a startling train of events.

The impulse to go into Bartletts' sweet shop that afternoon was instantaneous. During the war, sweets and chocolate were not easy to come by and Harriet took that sudden step into the shop thinking that the sweets would be a treat for the children when they came that weekend.

She passed the shop every day, sometimes stopping for chocolate for her mother or tobacco for her father and she had got to know Amy and to like her. She knew enough to know that Amy's mother did not live at home but looked after old Mrs Bartlett above the shop.

As Harriet had stepped into the shop, she had been startled to hear shouting in the room behind the shop. It was a male voice, deep, sonorous but at the same time sounding very irritated and cross. When the tall man had appeared from the back, he was immediately recognisable as Amy's father, they were so alike. Harriet found herself looking into dark eyes which were, just at that moment, bright with anger from his recent encounter.

Harriet was tall but she found herself having to look up to the handsome face confronting her. She had been made to drag her eyes away from his gaze and she felt a shiver go through her from the sensational impact with this person who seemed to be willing her to look into his eyes.

At last she dragged her gaze away and she heard the deep voice again, this time not raised in anger but resonant and sensuous, compelling and persuasive. Amy made the introductions and Harriet found herself putting her hand into his, the firm clasp sending further shivers through her. It was with a sense of relief that she heard him say that he had business in the town and with all the command she could muster, she had completed her purchases.

Once outside the shop, she strode purposefully up towards the town bridge, clutching her bags of sweets. She knew something of Daniel Holley but had never seen him before. Her father had some dealings with him as both were keen collectors of Worcester porcelain, but the man she had just met seemed to bear no relationship to the man who was the collector, the owner of the sweet factory, the father of Amy and the subject of local gossip because his wife did not live at home.

Harriet shook her head as though she was trying to throw off the feelings which were still dominated by the feel of his strong grasp of her hand and the look in his eyes. She knew admiration when she saw it but it was more than that. It was a look in which she had almost drowned and one which she had wanted to go on for ever.

As she walked briskly along, it was almost as though a small earthquake had erupted inside her. She stopped at the bridge and looked into the quiet waters of the river. The bewildering sensations ebbed and she began to think and feel normally again. After all, what had happened except that she had gone into a small sweet shop and met someone to whom she was instantly attracted.

She crossed to walk up to Regent Square but she did not bother to look for wagons or carts as it was usually quiet just there. She had scarcely reached the paving stones on the other side of the road when a pony and trap swung round from Bridge Street and the off-side wheels just brushed against her coat sleeve as it passed. She stumbled on to the pavement but did not fall.

Jolted out of her dream world, she looked up angrily to see who could have taken the corner so sharply and almost knocked her over. The trap had drawn up and a man had jumped down, running quickly towards her. Harriet just could not believe her eyes. It was as though she herself had conjured up the figure from her musings of the last few minutes. It was Daniel Holley and he was nearly at her side.

'Miss Bray.'

She could not look at him, could not trust herself to look into those eyes again.

'Miss Bray, do forgive me. We came down the hill rather fast and I was sure that you were going to reach the pavement in time. Are you all right? You were walking rather slowly. Are you unwell? Let me take your arm.'

She was glad of his words. It gave her time to pull herself together. She would not be intimidated by this man.

'Thank you, Mr Holley. The wheel hardly touched me. I am quite all right.'

She found herself looking up at him involuntarily. The penetrating gaze was still there but this time it held kindness and concern.

'I was very pleased to meet you this afternoon. Do you go into the shop very often?'

His tone was polite and she felt it would be churlish not to reply.

'I do go in occasionally to buy chocolate for my mother though of course, lately, it hasn't been so easy to come by.'

'No, it has been a difficult time. But it's amazing what you can do by making each sweet a little bit smaller and I don't think anyone has noticed.'

Thinking what an odd conversation this was, Harriet smiled. And Daniel smiled back. His smile was radiant, lighting his eyes with a quality that made her feel that the smile was for her alone. It also made her wary and she started to hesitate and to make excuses.

'I must be on my way home, Mr Holley,' she said. 'My mother will be wondering what has become of me.'

She turned as though to walk up Bridge Street but Daniel made a gesture towards the trap.

'Please, let me drive you home, Miss Bray. It's the least I can after almost knocking you over.'

But Harriet once more had possession of herself and replied firmly.

'No, thank you. I only have to walk up Bridge Street and I shall be home.'

She was thankful that he did not press her but gave a slight bow and another smile.

'Goodbye then, Miss Bray. Perhaps one day we shall meet under more formal circumstances.'

Harriet walked on up the hill. She was unable to put the astonishing encounter from her mind. To meet this man twice within an hour must be more than coincidence. Was fate playing with her life and her emotions, she wondered.

When she reached home, Harriet found her mother in the drawing-room.

Mrs Bray was seated in front of a brightly burning log fire. Even though seated, it was evident she was a tall woman. Dressed in severe black, her face was forbidding, with no softness or lines of love. Like her husband, she was a strict disciplinarian.

Mrs Bray turned as Harriet entered.

'Hello, Harriet. I thought you would never come. I'm afraid I've got another headache.'

Harriet sighed. Her mother had no worries, very few responsibilities, a fine home and a good husband. She liked to imagine herself an invalid but as she was strong and had no physical ailment, she produced her fragile nerves to draw attention to herself.

'I'm sorry, Mother,' Harriet said. 'I'll get you something.'

'Thank you, dear. Now, I will have some tea sent in as there is something I wish to tell you.'

As Harriet drank her tea, she put her own problems from her mind and waited. She was slightly puzzled as she thought her mother seemed nervous.

'Harriet, we have a guest coming for dinner tonight,' she said eventually.

Harriet looked up sharply. It was unusual for her parents to entertain and even more unusual that she should be told about the event so formally. An uneasy suspicion crossed her mind and she braced herself.

'Your father's partner and colleague, Mr Strickland, has been good enough to ask for your hand in marriage and is coming to see you tonight.'

Harriet swallowed hard. Even though her suspicion had been right, it did not stem the red hot flood of rebellion that swept through her. This the 20th century! She was an educated, emancipated, young woman who would soon be able to vote. The protective and possessive attitude of her parents was sometimes hard to bear, but what could she say to her mother without upsetting them completely?

'Mother, you know, because we have talked about it before, that I do not wish to be married. I have my career and I am quite happy as I am.'

'But, dear, Mr Strickland would be such a good husband for you. He has a fine house, he and your father are close colleagues and we know what a respected, upstanding man he is. He admires you tremendously and spoke of you in very favourable terms to your father.'

Harriet thought she would scream, but she clenched her fists, shut her eyes and tried to think how she could best put her feelings. Mr Strickland was younger than her father though his partner in business, but he was over fifty and had been a bachelor all his life.

She almost shuddered as she thought of him. He was the same height as herself but rotund, balding, precise and pompous with little, fat white hands that he pressed together as he talked. Because of his relationship with her father, he always assumed a false air of familiarity with her. She had never liked him and the thought of marriage to him was nothing short of repugnant to her.

'I'm sorry, Mother, if it offends you but I have no intention of marrying Mr Strickland,' she said.

'I sincerely hope, my dear Harriet, that between now and dinner, you will have thought seriously about your decision and will have a different reply to give to Mr Strickland.'

Nothing her mother said was going to make Harriet change her mind and she got up without another word and went up to her room to change. Dinner was at eight. She knew her father had come home from his office but she had neither seen him nor spoken to him.

She heard Mr Strickland arrive as she put the finishing touches to her hair. She regarded her looks in the mirror. If anyone had told her she was beautiful, she would have been amused, but her looks pleased her and tonight she was wearing a high-collared dress of soft, sand-coloured velvet, blending with the colour of her eyes and her hair into an attractive picture.

She walked slowly downstairs having thought no more about the answer she was going to give Mr Strickland as her mother had instructed. She had no need to. Her mind was made up and she was certain that she would rather stay a spinster than marry someone like Mr Strickland.

She could hear voices coming from the drawing-room and knew that she would have to join them all for sherry before dinner was served. As she walked across the room to shake hands with Mr Strickland, she could sense her father nodding in approval. He was proud of his daughter. She placed her hand in the soft, plump white one and could hardly bear the feel of the limp flesh. Mr Strickland was smiling at her with self-satisfaction as well as with admiration and she guessed that her parents had led him to believe that their daughter would one day become his wife.

The talk before dinner was general and Harriet was thankful when the move was made into the dining-room. Sitting around the table and being served with the excellent food which Mrs Bray's cook had succeeded in producing in spite of the food shortages, it was easier to keep up a flow of general conversation.

As they rose from the table to take coffee in the drawing-room, the dreaded moment arrived. Her parents had gone ahead when Mr Strickland put his hand on Harriet's arm to detain her in the dining-room. She drew herself up to her full height to give herself confidence and the feeling that she was looking down on him.

'Miss Bray,' he said, 'you must be aware of the great esteem in which I hold you. It would be foolish to pretend that I am in the first flush of youth but I believe it is true to say that I have the qualities of maturity and self-possession which many younger men may lack.

'I can also offer you a fine life-style

and a splendid house on the outskirts of the town where I now reside. I also intend to buy a motor car and if you married me, you would be a lady of the first fashion in the town.'

How to stop his flow of words she did not know but she felt that in the first short pause that it was necessary to give him some hint that she was by no means agreeable to his proposal.

'Mr Strickland, you are very kind but I think it only fair to tell you that I am not contemplating marriage at this moment.'

Her words seemed to delight Mr Strickland.

'My dear Miss Bray, I would not dream of rushing you into marriage. I know how few years it is since your sad bereavement. But your parents have assured me that they would like to see you married and that they look upon me as a suitable partner in life for you.'

Any inner amusement that had been gathering in Harriet was replaced at these words by a spasm of anger at her parents and this now escaped from her, directing itself towards the unfortunate Mr Strickland. She stepped towards the door, fighting for polite words and hardly succeeding.

'Mr Strickland, I must tell you that my parents do not make my decisions for me nor will I have them rule my life. I have made up my mind and nothing you say will change it. I will never marry you, never. Good-night.'

She left him standing, protesting, red in the face but she did not care. She snatched up an old cloak from the hall-stand and rushed out of the front door, running out of the house.

Anger lengthened her stride as she crossed the square but as it subsided and her thoughts became more rational, she walked more slowly. The enormity of what her parents had done was incomprehensible to her. How could they have told Mr Strickland that she would marry him? It was like a story out of another century.

She had hardly noticed where she had walked but looking up she found herself crossing to the riverside almost in the same place where she had met Daniel Holley that afternoon. The thought of him and the comparisons between the two men sobered her and she put her hand against the rail overlooking the water to steady herself.

There was a keen river breeze blowing up from the sea and she put the hood of her cloak over her head to give herself some protection. As her hand touched her cheek, she felt a wetness. Tears had come unannounced and for the first time in all those years she felt forlorn.

'Miss Bray.'

Harriet jumped round, frightened and startled by the sound of her name coming in the darkness — and it was a voice that could only have come from one person. Anger was in her voice for the second time that evening.

'Daniel Holley? You again? Are you haunting me? To meet you once in this place might have been a coincidence but what does it mean that you are here again and just when I wished to be private, too?'

The tall figure stood straight and serious at her side.

'Miss Bray, you are upset. A young girl like you should not be out on her own at night.'

His voice showed concern, almost anxiety. But Harriet was still startled and angry at the unexpected encounter.

'I do not have to explain my actions to you, Mr Holley,' she said.

'Listen to me if you can, and perhaps you will understand. This afternoon our meeting here was not a coincidence. Having met you in the shop, I just felt I had to see you again. I drove round and round until you appeared and then I nearly knocked you over! That was an accident, I can assure you. But not tonight. It must be fate that has brought us together again at this spot.

'I was restless at home and had a

sudden fancy to re-visit the place where I had spoken to you this afternoon. It was with the utmost astonishment and a certain unease on your behalf that I realised that the cloaked figure leaning over the rail was you. But you have not told me why you are here. I know it is none of my business but it is not safe for you to be out alone at this time of night.'

By this time they were both leaning over the rail. The only light came from the sky, the moon, partly hidden by racing clouds, casting a gentle glimmer over the water. The town was silent and dark and not a single person moved through the streets.

Harriet was gathering together her disordered thoughts. Was there no end to the complications of this day? She felt drawn to this man and felt an inexplicable urge to tell him of her troubles. His next question made her think that he must have been reading her very thoughts.

'I can see you are troubled,' he said

40

quietly. 'Would you like to tell me about it? Perhaps I might be able to help you.'

She gave a soft laugh.

'I think that just meeting you has put things into perspective. It all seems quite extraordinary. It was just a slight argument with my parents. They had invited a friend of theirs to dinner and told him that I would be willing to marry him. He's old and fat, and, oh, dear, I shouldn't be telling you all this. It's betraying a confidence.'

'It is safe with me. I think you needed to talk to someone. As I understand it, you have refused to marry this man?'

'Of course, I have. I couldn't marry anyone I did not love.'

She stopped horrified, remembering who it was by her side and the stories she had heard about his marriage.

'You don't have to stop. I know what you are thinking. Love can change, you know, or perhaps you are too young to know.'

She glanced sideways at his serious face.

'No, I am not too young. And I thought I loved my fiancé before he was killed at the beginning of the war but now I am not at all sure. It doesn't seem real any more. And . . . '

She hesitated. She must stop thinking about her parents and certainly not talk about them to this stranger.

'And what, Harriet?'

His use of her first name seemed to drop entirely naturally between them.

'I was thinking, as I walked down here, I don't really feel as though I love my parents. They seemed like strangers to me tonight.'

'No, we all have a duty to our parents but it is a different kind of love. Believe me, you will find true love one day.'

But Harriet shook her head.

'No, sometimes I think it has passed me by. I must resign myself to being an old maid.'

Daniel laughed.

'You a spinster? That is never your fate in life. And I think that fate has been playing tricks with us today. Did you not feel something when we met this afternoon? And now comes this further meeting, so unexpected and somehow so important. It makes me wonder if your fate is somehow linked with mine.'

She thought of the emotion when their eyes had first met but could only speak with astonished dismay.

'Mr Holley, I don't know what you can mean. You are a married man, with a wife and children. We are never likely to meet again.'

Daniel shook his head.

'I will not believe that. I will not believe that I have met you this one day never to meet again. I don't begin to understand it, but somewhere, somehow, we will meet again. And it won't be in this clandestine way. It will be in proper company when we can talk and laugh and look into each other's eyes again.'

She moved away from the rail.

'Mr Holley, I think we must forget this last hour. You have been most kind but I should not be here with you and we must think of it as something that has happened in our imagination and fancy. I am going home now. Goodbye.'

'Put your hood over your face, Harriet, and wrap your cloak around you. No-one would know you, and I insist on walking home with you.'

Harriet started to protest but she knew it would be useless against the will of this man. They walked in total silence and when they reached the square, Daniel paused for a moment at the door of the Bray house. He bent his head towards her and whispered words which Harriet only just caught and when she heard them, she could not truly believe them.

'Good-night, Harriet, my dear. I will see you again, one day.'

He disappeared into the night then and she let herself silently into the house hoping to avoid her parents. But when she stepped into the hall it was to find her mother standing at the foot of the stairs, menacing and disapproving.

'Harriet, wherever have you been?' she asked frostily. 'You have been gone for over an hour and it is dark. Have you no concern for your father and me at all?'

Harriet was not prepared to argue and stood silent, wishing that she could squeeze past her mother and rush up the stairs to the sanctuary of her room. But the tirade had not yet finished.

'You must know that you left Mr Strickland a very disappointed man. He was very concerned when you ran off, as any decent man would have been. He even walked round the square to see if he could find you. As for your behaviour, your father and I feel mortified, we invited Mr Strickland here . . . '

But Harriet could stand no more. Words burst from her and they, too, were icy.

'Mother, I am sorry if I have upset you but you are treating me like a child. When I decide to get married, it will be my choice. You and father have each other. If you would prefer not to be saddled with a spinster daughter, then I will seek a lodging elsewhere. That is all I have to say. Good-night.'

'I'm sorry, Harriet. We thought . . . '

Mrs Bray was not allowed to continue as Harriet started up the stairs.

'Good-night, Mother,' she repeated.

Harriet composed herself until she reached her room but once in its familiar comfort, she collapsed into her chair, the cloak still wrapped around her. Her brain reeled with the conflicting emotions of the day and of the last hour. She felt dismay tinged with an inexplicable fascination from the encounter with Daniel Holley and as the turbulent feelings seethed within her, she gave way at last to the relief of tears.

The outburst was violent and short

and Harriet was once again in command
of herself. She took off her cloak, made
herself a hot drink on the small gas-ring
she had in her room, sat down in the
easy chair by the fire and gave herself
up to thoughts of her present dilemma
and to memories of the past.

3

The whole family went to see Percy off at the railway station and when they returned home they were surprised to see the front door of the house in Rhodes Place standing open. Amy ran up the path to see what was happening. There was no sound to be heard but in the hall she stood with a puzzled frown. The Chinese vase that was always to be found on the hall table was upside down, the landscape in oils at the bottom of the stairs was turned to the wall.

She started to grin and looked in the sitting-room. She was right! All the pictures in there were face to the wall and she gave a whoop of delight.

It meant only one thing and that was that George was home! George, her big sailor brother, her partner in many pranks and much mischief, was home from the sea. When he came into the house on leave, the first thing he did was to turn all the pictures back to front. She knew he was hiding from them.

'George,' she shouted, running through the house. 'Where are you? You needn't hide! We'll soon find you.'

Edmund and Frank joined in the hunt and with great shouts of glee eventually dragged George from the cellar. Amy gave him a big hug. While all the shrieking was going on, Daniel came in the front door. He stood quietly for a moment, then a deep, enlightened laugh escaped from him.

'That noise means only one thing,' he said. 'George is home! Where are you, lad?'

There were hugs and talks and excitement all round. Unlike Edmund and Frank who were both tall, George was short and stocky, but what he lacked in height, he made up for in strength.

They were all talking at once as Mrs Chidgey brought a big tray of tea and cakes through from the kitchen. They all crowded into the sitting-room chattering and eating at the same time. George had been on the North Atlantic convoys which had struggled to escort the merchant ships bringing food into Britain, with much threat and danger from German submarines. The family hadn't seen him for over a year so there was a lot to tell.

When Edmund and Frank had gone up to bed and Daniel, as usual, into the drawing-room, George and Amy sat close to the fire and poured their hearts out to each other. The had always been close, with only just over a year between them.

'What shall we do tomorrow, Amy?' George asked.

'But, George, it's the Fair! Had you forgotten?'

George had dark curly hair which he ruffled now with his hands.

'I've lost track of the time. Is it the

last Wednesday in September?'

'Yes, of course it is and I shall be on our stall. Dad always shuts the shop on Fair days.'

Waterbridge Fair was an ancient one and not even a war could stop it even though the amusements and rides would be fewer than usual. Her mother usually helped Amy on the stall which was set up in the main street but she had decided it would be too much for her this year and Daniel had asked Mrs Chidgey to help, much to that lady's delight.

George helped them set up the stall with its sweets and gingerbread and then left Amy and Mrs Chidgey and wandered off in the direction of the fairground.

Amy was proud of him as he disappeared into the crowds. He was still in his naval uniform and looked youthful and handsome.

For two days, the stall was very busy particularly on early closing day when Daniel himself came to help. Amy was so occupied she hardly noticed whom she was serving and was surprised to hear a quiet voice say, 'Hello, Amy.'

She looked up to see Miss Bray standing at the stall with another lady and some children.

'This is my sister and my nieces and nephews.'

Harriet broke off as Daniel came and stood by Amy's side. Amy watched as the teacher's brown eyes glowed as she gave Daniel a lovely smile.

'Miss Bray,' he was saying, 'I am delighted to meet you again. Please, let me give you some sweets for the children.'

Still looking at him, Harriet shook her head.

'Oh, no, Mr Holley, but it is very kind of you. We will buy them some gingerbread.'

But while she was speaking, Daniel had begun to put some orange and lemon slices into paper bags and each child happily received their little gift. As the family party moved off in the direction of the Fair Field, Amy looked up and was startled to see the look on her father's face. His eyes followed the group as they walked up the High Street but she knew instinctively that the expression of soft tenderness she had never before seen in his eyes must have been for Harriet alone.

Amy felt the same perplexity that she had experienced when Daniel and Harriet had met in the shop but she also felt that here were things beyond her understanding and she put the two of them out of her mind and concentrated on the business of selling the fairings. By tea-time, Daniel said that he and Mrs Chidgey could manage on their own and Amy set off with George to see something of the fair.

They entered the Fair Field and joined the crowds enjoying themselves there. Amy wanted to try everything including the helter skelter and she came down in a whoosh of flying skirts. Amy couldn't drag George away from the side-shows. She hated them and when he insisted on going in to see the Heaviest Girl in the World, she flatly refused.

'I'll have a turn on the hoopla while you go in,' she told him.

They all enjoyed George's brief stay at home and Amy was sad to see him go back. It was then she realised just how much she was missing Percy. Now back in the shop each day and nowhere to go in the evenings, life was becoming very dull indeed.

After she shut up the shop of an evening, she had taken to having tea with her mother and Grandma Bartlett before going home. There had been fewer arguments of late between Dorrie and Daniel and Amy thought that Dorrie seemed more cheerful. But sometimes when Amy saw her mother's dark eyes and thin, drawn face, she had the feeling that Dorrie was more ill than any of them imagined.

Amy brought all her sewing to Grandma Bartlett and they would spend a long time looking through the fashion books. All she knew about dress-making, Amy had learned from her grandmother and she had been delighted when, a few months earlier, Mrs Bartlett had offered to teach her to make hats. Amy found she had a real talent and started to dream about becoming a milliner one day. One evening she mentioned it to her grandmother.

'Grandma, do you think I could become a milliner, after the war?'

The old lady smiled at the eager, young face. She didn't want to discourage her but she did not see how it would be possible in a town the size of Waterbridge.

'I don't know, dear,' she replied. 'There's no doubt that you have a flair and it's a pity to waste a gift like that but there isn't a proper milliner's in Waterbridge for you to get a training.'

Amy's face wore a slightly rebellious expression.

'But I don't especially want to stay in Waterbridge. I'd like to go away and work in a big city, like Exeter or Bristol.'

This last remark seemed to have set Mrs Bartlett thinking.

'I'll tell you what, Amy. I've an old school friend who has a smart milliner's shop in Bristol. If you like, I'll write and ask her if she needs an apprentice or even a girl to help in the shop.'

Amy threw her arms round the old lady.

'Oh, it would be wonderful, a real chance.'

She turned to her mother who had been listening keenly.

'What do you think about it, Mother?'

For once in her life, Dorrie was quite forceful.

'I think it's the best thing that could happen to you — give you a good chance in life. You might even end up with a shop of your own. Why don't you ask your father what he thinks?'

Amy smiled.

'Yes, I will,' she replied. 'This very evening.'

At Rhodes Place, not long after this conversation had taken place, Amy went in search of her father. She paused at the drawing-room door, hesitating to interrupt his quiet moments but when he saw her he smiled warmly and beckoned her to his side.

'My, Amy wants something,' he said with a touch of cheerful understanding.

'Well, yes, Dad, I do but I don't know how to ask you,' she said to him.

'Why don't you tell me the whole story from beginning to end?'

Amy pulled up her favourite, little stool and the whole tale was told. He listened quietly and patiently, nodding occasionally and puffing at his pipe.

'So, the sweet shop has got too small for our Amy, has it?'

'It's not that I dislike the shop, Dad, but I've been there since I left school and all through the war and now I'm eighteen I feel I could be doing a bit more with my life. I'm not looking down on the shop, Dad, please don't think that but it would be lovely to be doing something really creative. Do you understand how I feel?'

He placed an affectionate hand on her shoulder.

'Amy, my dear, I think I understand more than you would ever realise.'

She looked up in surprise and let him continue.

'When I left school, I was expected to go into my father's butcher's shop to learn the trade and I did. Then after Father died and left me his money, I came down here and married your mother. But I had to do the only thing I knew and that was to run a business. That's what I did and I have had enough success over the years to indulge in the things I love in life.'

'You mean the porcelain and the silver?'

'Yes, I do, love. And now that I've had my opportunities nothing will stop me letting my children going the way they wish to do.'

'Oh, Dad, do you mean you will let

me be a milliner?'

'Amy, if you feel you have a talent for making hats, you shall make hats.'

Amy rose to her feet.

'Now don't start getting excited before you hear what I have to say. If Mrs Bartlett thinks you have a gift for millinery then I believe it's only right and proper to use any gifts that God has given us. But, Amy, I would not like you to go away to be an apprentice, not even as near as Bristol.'

Amy's face fell in disappointment and she protested.

'But, Dad, girls go away to train for careers now. Look at Miss Bray.'

She stopped as an unusual look crossed her father's face.

'What's the matter? You remember Miss Bray, don't you? I introduced you to her in the shop and you saw her on Fair Day last week.'

As she spoke, she remembered the look on his face as his eyes followed the Bray family up the street.

'Do you like Miss Bray, Dad?'

As soon as the words were out she regretted them. He was nearly struggling for words.

'Harriet?'

The use of Harriet's first name surprised Amy but Daniel did not seem to notice and made his reply without any embarrassment.

'Yes, Amy, I do. I like her very much. I think she's a beautiful, young woman, and I am sure she is an excellent teacher.'

'That's just what I mean,' Amy cried out. 'I know she went to a London college to train as a teacher. She told me so once. Why can't I go away like she did?'

'Amy, I am being selfish. I just don't want to lose you. But there is an alternative, you know.'

'What's that?'

'Would you like me to buy you a shop of your own in Waterbridge and set you up as a milliner?'

'Dad, you can't mean it.'

'I do. There is no milliner in the

60

town and I think we could run a very successful, little shop. After all, anyone can run a sweet shop but it takes skill to be a milliner. What do you say, then?'

Amy's eyes were shining but at the back of her radiant expression, there was a little troubled frown.

'There's something wrong, isn't there, Amy? What have you thought of now?'

'Well, it's a wonderful idea, Dad, and very generous of you but you see, I'm not a milliner yet. I've only made two hats. Grandma Bartlett thinks I would be good at it but that's all. I still need to go away and work in a proper milliner's to learn the trade. Don't you think I am right?'

'Yes, I suppose you are so why don't we make a bargain?'

'A bargain?'

'Yes, when the war is over, we'll get Mrs Bartlett to write to her friend in Bristol and see if she'll have you to work in her shop for a while then when you feel you have learned enough, you can come home and we'll look for a little shop here.'

Amy gave her father an enormous hug.

'You are a dear, kind father and I thank you. I wouldn't mind coming back to Waterbridge and living with you all again. You mustn't think I want to leave you, but it would be wonderful to think that one day I might have a shop of my own. I've never wanted anything so much in all my life, except . . . '

She stopped abruptly.

'Well, there is one other thing but I'm not telling you yet because I am sure you will laugh and say no.'

Daniel gave a half-groan.

'Not some other madcap scheme of yours and whenever have I been known to refuse you anything?'

They both laughed and Amy kissed him and thanked him again before going up to bed.

The dull despondency of the beginning of that week had changed to one of optimism for Amy; Mrs Bartlett was told of Daniel's plan and she promised to write to her milliner friend in Bristol when the time came.

Then came Saturday morning and an incident which sent Amy's spirits soaring. It was the custom for Dorrie to look after the shop while Amy went to the bank to pay in the week's takings. Amy always enjoyed this little mission. Mr Bird, the bank manager, knew Daniel well and had a soft spot for Amy.

Entering the big doors of the solemn building, Amy immediately looked for Mr Bird but he was not in his usual place. As she walked up to the counter where she paid in the money, she was surprised to find a stranger sitting there. His dark head was bent over rows of figures and in the seconds before he looked up, Amy had time to wonder who this young man could be. She had never seen him before.

Then, as he looked up and saw her standing there, she was filled with a sensation she had never experienced in the whole of her life. The face that was looking at her was very pale and it was also thin and serious, but as he saw the pretty, young girl in front of him, his expression changed. His mouth curved in a slight smile and the smile lit up the blue-grey eyes that were regarding her — eyes that changed the hollow strain of the face into one of attractive, mesmeric shyness and interest.

Amy felt a flutter not only in her heart but through her body as though it was shooting right down to her toes. All these sensations occurred in the short time it had taken her to lift up her bags of cash and to put her book in front of the young man. As she did so, she noticed his name lettered in gold by the side of his hand — Mr John Tottle.

Just as she was thinking about the name and the significance of the fact that there was a new cashier in the bank, Mr Bird came up beside her.

'Hello, Miss Holley. I must introduce

you to my new cashier. John, this is Miss Amy Holley, the daughter of my good friend Daniel Holley, with whom we do a good deal of business.'

Amy looked embarrassed but John Tottle's shy smile broadened into a generous grin.

'I'm very pleased to meet you, Miss Holley.'

His voice was formal but the firm softness of it took the edge off the formality and gave both his look and his words a feeling of sincerity. Amy hardly knew what to say and the words, when they came, seemed trivial.

'I come in every Saturday morning, Mr Tottle.'

As his eyes met hers she felt that same thrill of pleasure.

'I shall be very pleased to see you, Miss Holley.'

Amy gathered up the book and the now-empty cash bags and said a quick goodbye. It was accompanied by a radiant smile which was returned by the young man behind the counter.

She walked down Eastfield in a dream. She tried to keep before her mind's eye the good-looking, young face, the dark hair and the warmth of the smile in his eyes.

4

A chill October wind faced Harriet as she walked home from school about a month later. Since the brief meeting on Fair Day, she had not seen Daniel Holley but not a day went past without her thinking of him.

On school days, she walked up Eastfield and approached Bartlett's shop with a nervous anticipation in case she should meet him there. The trepidation in her step spoke of the feeling of dread that she might see him and have to speak to him but at the same time there was a conflicting feeling of keen expectation which she knew to be wrong.

Nothing more had been said at home on the subject of Mr Strickland and Harriet spent most of her time in her room. As the weeks passed, the tensions began to ease.

That cold day with autumn soon to change to winter, Harriet had had a tiring day and looked forward to a quiet evening in her room, reading and perhaps doing some embroidery which she found relaxing.

Mrs Bray was in the drawing-room and she jumped up in her chair at Harriet's entrance.

'Hello, Mother, are you all right? You seem rather on edge.'

'Harriet,' she said in a tone that sounded rather flustered. 'Harriet, I have something to tell you. We have a guest for dinner tonight.'

Harriet's heart plummeted. They were never matchmaking again already, were they? Hadn't she made it clear what her feelings on the subject were?

'Mother . . . '

'Don't interrupt me, Harriet. The guest tonight is a friend of your father's and is coming to do some business with him but I would like to think that you would be present for I am sure that Mr Holley would like to meet you.'

There was a stunned silence and Harriet was rooted to the spot. The astonishment must have been written clearly on her face as her mother started to speak rather anxiously.

'What is the matter, Harriet? Do you . . . '

She got no further for Harriet had at last found her voice.

'Mr Holley, did you say, Mother?'

'Yes, dear.'

'Mr Daniel Holley?'

'I've no idea what his first name might be, Harriet. It is no concern of mine. Do you know a Mr Holley then?'

Harriet had committed herself now but tried to retract.

'I don't think it can be the same person. The Mr Holley I was introduced to would not, I think, be coming to dinner in this house.'

She was furiously thinking to herself. Whatever shall I do if it is him? Her thoughts were so muddled that she only heard the end of her mother's next remark.

'Something to do with Worcester porcelain.'

The few words were enough to give Harriet an inward sigh of relief. It wasn't Daniel! It was one of her father's old collector cronies. They sometimes came to buy or perhaps exchange a valuable piece of china with something from Mr Bray's own collection.

'I will go and change and rest now, Mother, and then I will be down in good time for dinner.'

The conversation in the drawing-room had disturbed Harriet. She sat in her room trying, not for the first time, to sort out her thoughts and feelings. Daniel Holley seemed to have come into her life, then to have left it but not without the endless possibility that she might meet him again. She was too unsure of her own reaction to his dynamic presence.

As soon as the war is over, she thought for the hundredth time, I will try to get a headship in the country and distance myself from this town and its inherent dangers.

She made herself some tea and then set about slowly and quietly dressing for dinner. Even if the guest was her father's age, she felt she owed it to her parents to look her best.

By half-past six, she was ready and as she heard the sound of the front door opening and closing, she knew that the guest must have arrived. Knowing that he would be in the drawing-room and thinking it only polite to join him, she made her way slowly downstairs. In the hall, she met her mother looking rather harassed.

'Harriet, your father is seeing to the sherry and cook wishes to speak to me urgently. Could you go and keep Mr Holley company for a few minutes? Your father will soon be along.'

Harriet nodded and turned into the drawing-room. Her suspicions had been lulled, her suspecting mind had been assured, the doubts and fancies had been crushed. But as she came into that room, they all came flowing back with a startling reality. There, standing with his back to the fireplace, was Daniel Holley. Harriet stood frozen in utter silence as Daniel spoke.

'Harriet.'

Harriet took a deep breath, feeling pleasure and joy, suspicion and disbelief, even anger. She did now know which feeling was uppermost.

'Daniel Holley, what are you doing here? How have you got the effrontery to come here to dinner?'

He took a step forward and cradled her hand in his.

'Harriet, my dear, you look . . . '

He let go of her hand suddenly and then took it up again as though shaking her by the hand.

'I'm delighted to meet you, Miss Bray,' he said.

'Ah, you have met my daughter, Holley.'

The reason for Daniel's sudden change of action was Mr Bray who had entered the room with glasses of sherry on a tray. Harriet shook with inward laughter, her indignation fled. This man was a rogue, but what a loveable rogue! She sat down and set herself to see what charm Daniel Holley had worked on her father to secure this invitation.

Mrs Bray joined them, flushed from her visit to the kitchen and conversation became general. It remained so throughout dinner but Harriet did discover one important clue to the guest's presence. Her mother had been correct. Daniel was, in fact, one of Mr Bray's collecting cronies and it was Worcester porcelain they both collected. But some wicked prompting made Harriet ask herself just how long Daniel had been collecting Worcester porcelain!

As they rose from the table to go into the drawing-room, Mr Bray put his arm round his daughter's shoulder, an unusual gesture and it served to outline his pleasure at his guest's company.

'Harriet, while we are waiting for the coffee to be served, why don't you take

Mr Holley to your sitting-room to see your books? Book-collecting is another of his hobbies and it is you who is the book-lover in this family.'

Harriet was astonished but very quick and very pleased to seize an opportunity to speak to Daniel for a few moments on his own.

'I would be delighted, Mr Holley, though I am sure that mine is a poor collection compared to yours.'

Daniel showed the same serious face that he had worn all the time he had been in her parents' company and as they climbed the stairs, Harriet found it difficult to keep her composure. She felt a mood of intrigue and hilarity bubbling up inside her which was quite foreign to her.

Inside the large room, she walked to the fire and then turned to her guest as he closed the door behind him. His face glowed with pleasure and his eyes, previously sober, lit up as he looked at her.

'Daniel, you have me bursting with

curiosity. However did you get my father to invite you to dinner? You are a rogue through and through. Sit down and tell me all the wickedness you have been planning.'

While she was speaking and taking a seat in the easy chair at the side of the fire, he leaned across the warmth of the fire and took her hand. She made a move to withdraw hers but the firmness of the clasp stopped her.

'Harriet, all I want to say is what I started to say when your father interrupted us, downstairs before dinner. You look beautiful. You are the loveliest person I have ever seen in my life.'

But Harriet was not to be impressed by flattery even though the words were spoken in utmost sincerity and she repeated her question. This time, Daniel released her hand and sat back in his chair and laughed.

'Harriet, it was so easy. In the first place, I was determined to see you in proper circumstances and I have to confess that I knew that your father collected Worcester porcelain, just as I do though I could see the doubt in your eyes. And it wasn't difficult to go to the sale room to buy a few pieces and to get him chatting on his favourite subject. From then on it was easy, and in a moment he will show me his collection and maybe I will add a piece to mine.'

'Are you really a collector, Daniel?'

'Why are you so surprised? You know nothing about me. You know nothing except that we looked into each other's eyes and a spark was struck. Can you deny it?'

She shook her head but looked at him steadily.

'You know that I must not recognise that spark, Daniel. You know that it cannot be.'

'But you are not going to deny me a few moments of your company under your parents' roof, are you?'

Harriet could only smile.

'I am being no more than a dutiful

daughter. And that reminds me that we came up here to look at my books. The bookcase is behind you. Which authors do you like, Daniel?'

She watched him as he got up to look at the books in the glass-fronted bookcase.

'Wordsworth, John Donne, Robert Herrick,' he replied.

'Poetry?'

'Yes. Why do you sound so surprised?'

He turned round to look at her.

'I don't think I am surprised that you read poetry. I am discovering new things about you every moment and I can imagine you delighting in Robert Herrick. But John Donne? Are you a religious man, Daniel?'

'If you mean by religious, do I attend service regularly and am I a pillar of the church, like your father, then the answer is no. But if on the other hand you are asking if I look for a spiritual answer to man's life, to man's destiny, to man's death, then the answer is yes. And the answers can be found in Donne and they can be found in Wordsworth.'

'I like Wordsworth, too,' she said softly.

'Oh, Harriet, we have so much in common and this is only a beginning.'

She gave herself an inward shake and tried to steer the conversation away from intimate things to something more matter-of-fact and sensible. But it was not as easy as she had thought. As she moved towards the door, he looked at her and walked towards her.

'And now, Miss Bray, I think we must go and drink our cold coffee.'

She was grateful for the change of mood.

'I don't know what my mother and father will be thinking, do you?'

He opened the door for her and bent to her ear.

'I don't really care, Harriet, and before we go down, I must tell you just one thing.'

There was an air of amusement in

his voice and she wondered what was coming next.

'And what is that, Daniel?'

'I don't collect books, my dear. Porcelain and silver, yes, but not books.'

Harriet shook with laughter.

'You're a rogue just as I said, Daniel Holley. There is no other word. But I won't tell Mother and Father. I've enjoyed this time with you and now we must return to the real world.'

Two weeks were to pass before Harriet saw Daniel again. In those two weeks, Amy made her plans for her adventure into millinery and during that time she saw John Tottle three times, on each occasion from the other side of the counter at the bank. She had a dream that he would walk into the shop one day and ask her to go for a walk but the dream never came true.

Monday, November 11, 1918, started as any other Monday. Harriet was back at school after two weeks' absence, because the schools in the town had been closed during an influenza epidemic. Both the Bray and the Holley family had managed to avoid the illness and in the shop that morning, Amy was arranging the jars of sweets. Her mother was upstairs helping Mrs Bartlett to get up and dress and to settle in her chair for the day.

Near enough to eleven o'clock, Amy paused in what she was doing and looked out of the door in amazement to see people running past. She could hear shouts and cries which became louder in the seconds it took her to open the door. Mystified, she went out into the street and just as it was beginning to dawn on her what was happening, she suddenly found herself picked up and given a big hug by none other than her father.

'Dad, put me down. Is it good news? Is the war over?'

Daniel was jubilant as he carried Amy into the shop and sat her on the counter as though she was a little girl.

'I've just heard,' he said. 'I ran all the way home to tell you. I've been at the Mercury Office since six o'clock this morning. Some have been there all night. A phone message has just been received. Yes, Amy, the war is over. The Armistice was signed at five o'clock this morning and all hostilities are to cease.'

Amy jumped down from the counter.

'Dad, you must go up and tell Mother and Grandma. I'll stay in the shop though we're not going to have any customers. Everyone is running up Eastfield. Look!'

Amy found it hard to contain her excitement and stood at the entrance to the shop as Daniel went upstairs to see Dorrie.

'Amy,' her father was calling and she ran back into the shop. 'Come along. We're going to shut the shop and go up to the Town Hall. Everyone is sure to be there.'

Daniel locked up the shop. The news was spreading like wildfire and as they

81

walked through the town, the sirens and hooters from the factories and the docks began to sound and the noise was deafening. It was obvious that work had stopped nearly everywhere. As Amy and Daniel crossed the town bridge, the sound of church bells rang out and they found that the main street was so congested that it was difficult to make any progress towards the Town Hall. Amy clung to Daniel as they were jostled and pushed from side to side.

'Dad, everyone is dancing,' she shouted above the noise and clamour.

'From the look of it, they've brought the piano from the Empire,' he said. 'Shall we join in, Amy?'

She shook her head at him and stayed at his side, content to stand and watch the joyful scene. After several minutes, Amy pulled Daniel's arm.

'Dad, there is Miss Bray. Look, over there. Can you see her?'

She made to move towards her, and Daniel was off across the road with

Amy. They reached Harriet's side and Daniel put his hand on her arm.

'Oh, Mr Holley,' she said. 'I couldn't be more pleased to see you. I know it sounds silly but I've lost Mother and Father in the crush. We were walking at the end of the procession and when we got to the crowd here, we were separated. I can't see them anywhere.'

Daniel's expression was one of amusement.

'My dear Miss Bray, I think your mother and father will be able to take care of themselves but I don't like to see you on your own. Why not stay with us? Someone has said that the mayor is going to make a speech.'

'Yes, thank you, I will stay with you and maybe I will find my parents there, too. And Amy, please call me Harriet. Miss Bray sounds so formal.'

Amy flushed with pleasure and took her father's arm again and they all walked to the Cornmarket where the mayor was getting ready to speak. They were standing near the bank when Harriet noticed a young man of her acquaintance coming down the steps. She also noticed that Amy was looking at him with an eager expression. When he saw Amy, he stopped and faltered but, sensing a slight awkwardness between the two young people, Harriet called out.

'John, have you only just left the bank? You are missing all the celebrations.'

John walked towards them but his eyes were on Amy. Harriet sought to make the introductions.

'Amy, this is John Tottle. His father is a teacher at school. John, may I introduce you to Miss Amy Holley, and her father, Mr Daniel Holley. Have you met before?'

Amy's smile was shy as she shook hands with the young man she had idolised for so long. She had not realised how very tall he would be.

'I have seen Mr Tottle in the bank,' she said.

The mayor gave his speech and there were cheers from the crowd when he announced that he had appealed to anyone who had businesses or factories to close them down for the day.

'Amy,' Daniel said, 'why don't you take John up to the square? He hasn't seen the dancing and the celebrations going on up there yet.'

Amy looked quickly from her father to John. Nothing would please her more but what would John think of the suggestion? There was an immediate response from him.

'That's a wonderful idea, Mr Holley, and then I will bring Amy home afterwards. Shall we go, Amy?' he said, taking her arm eagerly.

'Are you sure, Dad?' she asked.

Daniel replied before Harriet had a chance to say anything.

'I will take Harriet home,' he said, now formally polite. 'Her parents may be worrying.'

Amy looked relieved.

'That's all right then. Shall we go, John?'

The two young people disappeared into the crowd, leaving Harriet, exasperated, at Daniel's side.

5

There seemed to be rather a pleased smile on Daniel's face as Harriet turned to face him.

'Daniel Holley, you have done it again!' she said angrily.

'What have I done again, my dear Harriet?'

'I am not your dear Harriet and you know very well that you have manoeuvred the situation so that I am alone with you. And you know enough about me to realise that I would not think it correct for me to be seen out on my own with you.'

A wicked muscle twitched at the corner of Daniel's mouth.

'Very well, Miss Bray, there are two courses open to us to remedy the situation. First of all, I could leave you to fight your way through this unruly mob and to go home on your own. Or, secondly, we will find a quiet corner or a side street where there will be no people and my Harriet's sense of propriety will not be offended.'

'I am not your . . . '

She could not go on as she found laughter bubbling up inside of her.

'Oh, Daniel, you will always win, won't you? But this time I think I have beaten you. You will not be able to find a quiet corner in the whole of Waterbridge.'

'On the other hand, Harriet, I promised I would take you home. If you look round you will see that the whole of Waterbridge is here and if we go back to Regent's Square by way of the Court House, I think I can guarantee that we shall not see a soul.

'I can't win against you, Daniel, and somehow I don't think I want to try. You can take me home the quiet way.'

But Harriet felt uncomfortable as she walked stiffly by his side, hardly speaking. He looked at her set face.

'You are displeased with me, Harriet?' he said softly.

'I don't think that is quite the right word. It should not matter to you whether I am pleased with you or not.'

'But it does. Everything about you matters to me.'

Harriet felt close to tears.

'But, Daniel, it mustn't. It's not right and you know it.'

He slowed his step and his mood became serious.

'I'm sorry, Harriet. I have upset you and that was far from my intention. I was just so happy to have the chance of walking a few yards with you.'

Harriet's cheeks were moist and as Daniel came to a halt and she looked up at him, he put his fingers gently to her face to wipe away her tears. It was a soft gesture of loving care, a sensation that she knew was missing from her whole life. But Harriet managed to keep a check on her feelings and say the only words she knew it was possible to say.

'Daniel, would it make you happy to know that I feel the same? I cannot deny that I feel just as you do but I know that it is not right and I have thought and thought until my mind goes round in circles. And each time I can only come to one conclusion and I think it is one you will not like.'

'What do you mean, Harriet?'

His previously confident tone was tinged with doubts.

'I must not see you again. In the New Year, now that the war is over, I shall try to get a headship of a school somewhere away from Waterbridge and I will go out of your life.'

His hands clenched.

'I cannot bear it, Harriet. You have only just come into my life.'

'You will bear it because you know it is the right thing to do. I think you are an honourable person, Daniel.'

'I always thought I was but I've never felt like this before. Never before have

I felt this overwhelming yearning to be with a person. But, Harriet, I think that you have just shown me that you are indeed the wonderful person I thought you to be. If you choose to go away then I shall stand by you. Your happiness is what matters to me. I cannot offer you that happiness. But I can only let you go because of one thing that will sustain me.'

'And what is that, Daniel?'

'It is because I believe that our destinies lie together and not apart.'

He looked at the disbelief in her face.

'Harriet, I will say no more because I do not really understand it myself. I want your happiness more than anything. You may go your own way, and make a new life but nothing will ever break this link that has been forged between us.'

Relief showed in her eyes.

'Thank you, Daniel. Knowing that you understand and can feel like that will help me and I feel easier in my mind already.'

'Before we part, promise me one thing.'

'I cannot be sure,' she said in a voice filled with emotion.

'Yes, you must.'

He took both her hands and looked deep into her eyes.

'If ever you need me you will come for me.'

'Very well, Daniel.'

She made to part from him but he found it difficult to let her go. His eyes held hers with longing and there was deep feeling in his parting words.

'Goodbye, Harriet, and never forget one thing in all the life ahead of you. I love you, Harriet. I love you very much.'

His voice broke and he turned, leaving her standing in the quiet road watching his tall figure walk quickly back into the town. Dashing her hand across her eyes, she rushed to Regent's Square, let herself into the house and ran up to her room. She lay on her bed and cried and sobbed as though the world had forsaken her.

It was no comfort that she had said the right words, done the right thing, for she had denied herself a love she would never experience again for the rest of her life.

Meanwhile, Amy and John had made their way back to the Town Hall. The amazing scenes had become even more riotous, with dancers in old top hats and fancy dress dancing and waving and cheering. The pair had said very little as they concentrated on pushing their way through the crowds but as they stood watching the dancers, Amy glanced up at John. At the same moment, he looked down and their eyes locked in an unguarded moment. Amy felt a thrill but was lost for words. It was John who broke the silence.

'Do you like dancing, Amy?'

It was obvious from his tone that he did not and Amy was hesitant in giving a straight answer but she could never hide what she felt.

'Yes, I love dancing. It's my favourite

hobby. When my brother George is home, we go to the dances together and go in for competitions. You sound as though you don't like dancing though.'

There was a slight, awkward silence as though he desperately wanted to please her, to reassure her but he could not and he was almost apologetic.

'No, I have never been a dancer. I suppose I've always been too tall, and awkward,' he added, trying to laugh.

'I thought perhaps you had been injured at the Front. When I first saw you at the bank, you looked as though you had just come out of hospital.'

'No, it was nothing more than trench fever but it was bad enough to get me discharged. I'm better now and I've got my job back, too. Mr Bird has been very good to me.'

Amy was struggling to find something they might have in common.

'Have you got any hobbies?'

'Oh, yes,' was the confident reply from the young man. 'I love most sports, especially swimming and cricket.'

Amy's heart sank. She loathed the water and her brothers had never instilled in her their love of cricket. But she tried valiantly to answer him.

'Do you swim at the baths?'

'Yes. I'm in the water-polo team. Perhaps you would like to come and watch in the summer and cricket matches, too. I expect you would like cricket better.'

She would have to confess. She couldn't get off to a false start.

'I don't like cricket. I used to like bowling to my brothers on the vicarage field opposite us but I think a cricket match is boring.'

In the strained silence that followed she tried to retrieve herself.

'I think I would like watching water-polo even though I don't like swimming myself.'

Then, in her anxiety to please this young man, Amy blurted out something she had hidden deep in her heart all the war years and had told no-one.

'What I really want to do is to learn

to ride a motor-cycle. I've saved up enough to buy one.'

She looked at him triumphantly, only to find him looking at her with a deep frown.

'A motor-cycle? But girls don't ride motor-cycles. They are for men.'

Amy wasn't going to let John Tottle get away with this remark. She had both spirit and very definite ideas.

'Well, you're wrong and you should know. You were in the army. They had lady despatch riders. I know because Mr Brewer at the shop told me.'

'You mean the motor-cycle shop in Monmouth Road?'

'Yes, I do.'

Amy was on the defensive now and preparing herself for the next critical question.

'You've been to look at the motor-cycles in the workshop?'

'Yes, I have. Mr Brewer is a friend of mine. He does up old bikes and it means I could get one much cheaper than if I bought a new one. I think I shall have it after Christmas. I was just waiting for the war to finish. Don't you approve?'

John's face was a struggle of how to say exactly what he thought without upsetting Amy.

'Well, I can't say I do. There isn't a young lady riding a motor-cycle in Waterbridge and . . . '

He wasn't allowed to finish as Amy's pent-up enthusiasm burst out.

'I'm going to be the first one.'

John seemed to be at a loss for words. He touched Amy's arm and said, 'Do you think we should begin walking home now?'

At his words, Amy thought she had lost him. He would walk home with her and she would never see him again, except in the bank of course.

I must think of something to keep him, she thought in a panic. I can't lose him on the same day that I have found him. We must have something in common. Providence came to her rescue in the form of a large motor-car trying to edge its way through all the people.

'Of course,' she said with sheer bravado, 'if I had enough money I would buy a car.'

John's head turned to her like lightning, the disapproving look gone from his face to be replaced by one of eagerness and animation.

'Do you like cars? I drove one in France and I shall get one next year just as soon as I can manage it.'

He looked at her with great triumph and satisfaction in his eyes.

'Then I would be able to take you for rides into the country. Would you like that?'

Amy did like it, not just the idea of rides into the country but the startling fact that John was including her in his plans for the next year.

'Oh, yes, I would,' she replied with a brilliant smile. 'I love going into the country and up on the hills. Dad sometimes takes me in his trap.'

They had reached the river by now

and as they leaned over the bridge, they both felt happier.

'If you like the countryside, perhaps we could go for a walk one Sunday afternoon,' he said. 'Where we live there are some lovely walks.'

'Where do you live, John?'

'Out the Taunton road, in Broomfield Avenue.'

Their mood had changed and he started to tell her about his family, his father, a teacher, and his two elder brothers, both in business. Then he asked Amy about her family and by the time they reached Rhodes Place, they knew a little more about each other. They made arrangements to meet the following Sunday.

Amy went into the house feeling as though she had been skating on thin ice but had safely reached the other side of the lake! She couldn't resist telling Mrs Chidgey about John and she was soon asked the question she had been burying at the back of her mind.

'But what about Percy?' Mrs Chidgey asked.

Amy tried to appear untroubled.

'I didn't promise I'd wait for Percy and we don't know when he will be home. I've not even had a letter from him. In any case, John is not really my young man. We are only going for a walk and he doesn't like dancing.'

Mrs Chidgey couldn't help laughing.

'Miss Amy, you will have a queue of young men after you before you've finished! Now, it's not my place to say it but what about going to see your mother and your grandma? They would like to hear all about what's been going on.'

'Yes, I was going to go along to see them both,' Amy said. 'I just wanted to come and tell you about John first.'

Amy arrived at the shop to find her father sitting with Dorrie and Mrs Bartlett. She looked at him sharply as she entered the room. Gone was the buoyant look of earlier in the day. He was chatting easily enough to Dorrie but seemed distracted as though his mind was far away. But her mother seemed so pleased to see them.

The scenes in the town on that memorable day were described and Amy told her mother about John and his family. Dorrie seemed pleased. Afterwards, father and daughter walked back slowly to Rhodes Place and both of them seemed preoccupied. It was only as they were going into the house that Amy started to speak.

'Dad, I want to ask you about something.'

'What's that, my dear?'

Amy floundered.

'Well, John seemed to disapprove but I've made up my mind and I've got enough money . . . '

'Amy Holley, are you going to tell me what it is you want to ask me?' Daniel asked her with some amusement in his voice.

'I'm sorry, Dad. It's just that I'm nervous about asking you. Can I have a motor-cycle?'

'Oh, Amy.' Daniel sighed ruefully. 'You always were a bit of a tomboy. I suppose it comes from having three brothers. What a strange mixture you are. First a hat-shop and now a motor-cycle. I really don't know. I shall have to think about it.'

'I would be very careful, Dad, and it would only be a small one.'

Daniel gave a groan.

'I should hope not, but I think I would rather you had a car than a motor-cycle. Why not wait a little while and then perhaps next year we might think of getting a motor-car and we could both learn to drive it.'

Amy felt that it was going to be a hard fight to win the approval of anyone on the subject of the motor-cycle. First John and now her father disapproved and whatever would her mother say?

Christmas came and went for both Amy and Harriet. For the Holleys, Christmas Day was spent with Dorrie and Grandma Bartlett. They had sung carols and played cards and even Dorrie had been well enough to join in. Amy had Boxing Day to look forward to as John was coming to Rhodes Place to tea. She knew he was acquainted with her father but she wondered what her high-spirited brothers would make of the serious, young man.

She need not have worried. They immediately found that they had two interests in common — cricket and cars. Once these topics had been introduced, the conversation was well away and Amy was content to sit back and watch John enjoying himself with Edmund and Frank.

As the evening wore on, Amy realised that her father had come back from visiting Dorrie and was sitting in the drawing-room on his own. She and John joined him and he seemed pleased to see them.

'Would you like a game of cards, Dad?' Amy asked.

'No, thank you, my dear. I am feeling rather tired but don't let me stop you two from playing.'

She looked up at his face and noticed that the eyes were dark and that there were lines of strain about his mouth.

'Are you worrying about Mother?' she asked him. 'I though she seemed a little better yesterday.'

'Yes, Amy, I think she did and today we have had a game of cards again, and Mrs Bartlett, too. Now what about you and John? Would you like to play?'

Amy looked at John but he shook his head.

'No, thank you, Mr Holley. I think I must be on my way home.'

Amy looked disappointed but she was pleased at the success of the visit and jumped up and followed John to the door. In the dim light of the hall, she looked at John's face as he put on his coat. His expression was full of pleasure and apparent gladness and his words echoed the look on his face.

'Amy, it has been lovely to meet your family and to come to your house.

Thank you very much. It was the nicest part of Christmas for me.'

'I've enjoyed it, too, John.'

She held out her hand as though to shake hands on parting but he slowly took her hand and enfolded it in both of his. It was a gesture full of meaning and tenderness and brought a flush to Amy's cheeks.

'Amy, may I kiss you?' he asked, unsure and hesitant.

She didn't know what to say but the fact that she did not draw her hands away seemed to signal to him that she had consented. She was drawn against the thick wool of his winter coat and his arm cradled her against him. When he bent his head and touched her lips with his, the sensation through her whole body was electric. She found herself standing on tip-toe to return the kiss, wishing the moment would never end.

At last, with a sigh, John lifted his head. The emotional response from Amy had deprived him of words and he simply clutched her hands to him once more.

'Amy, thank you. I must go now.'

Amy was glad she had to say no more than, 'Goodbye, John,' as she, too, was overcome by the first appearance of passion in her young life.

Her father smiled when she went back into the room and seemed glad to exchange a few words with his young daughter.

'I must say I like your young man, Amy, and I believe he got on very well with Edmund and Frank.'

Amy screwed up her nose in mock disgust.

'Yes,' she said. 'They talked about cricket.'

Daniel's sober look was replaced with one of merriment.

'That's my Amy. Disapproves of her brothers' love of cricket and then tells me she wants a motor-cycle! Or have you forgotten that idea? Has John made you change your mind?'

'No, we didn't talk about it,' she

said. 'I'm still thinking it over.'

'Oh, well, we will see what the new year brings. Now, I don't know about you but I'm ready for bed, Amy. Are you going up now?'

'Yes, Dad, I am going up now.' Then she added quickly, 'I'm glad mother was better yesterday. She seemed much happier, didn't she?'

His look was unfathomable but his agreement was wholehearted and cheerful.

'Yes, we had a nice day. Good-night, my dear.'

6

That same Boxing Day, Harriet was dutifully playing whist with her parents and her aunt. She tried to make intelligent conversation, tried not to make too many mistakes in her game but it was not easy. She caught her mother looking at her sharply more than once.

She felt like screaming and running away from the card table and it was only by a supreme effort of willpower that she did not give way to her emotions. When it was time for her aunt to go home, she offered to accompany her across the square, glad of the excuse to be out in the fresh air with her thoughts. She said good-night to her aunt and it seemed automatic to venture down Bridge Street to the river. The waters, even after dark, seemed to have a calming effect.

With Christmas over, she knew the time had come for her to think seriously of leaving home and putting the emotional turmoil caused by the presence of Daniel Holley out of her life.

The first thing would be to try and get a school of her own. She would write to the Education Department straightaway. If only she could get a headship in a village school there would almost certainly be a school house or cottage to go with it.

She paused for a moment in her reasoning as a problem with this idea suddenly struck her. It would be all very nice to be out in the country but how would she get there? Rural villages were not often served by trains and she had no transport of her own.

Looking up the river, she was suddenly aware of the headlights of a motor car making its way over the bridge and that gleam of light in the darkness seemed in a flash to solve all Harriet's problems. She would get a small motor car! With an excited impulse, she turned away from the river and started to walk quickly up Bridge Street. Loving Daniel could bring nothing but heartbreak and she was determined to put her feelings behind her.

Harriet found her parents in the sitting-room when she returned to the house.

'I want to talk to you both,' she said as she joined them. 'I've been doing a lot of thinking and now that the war is over, I want to do something that I have had in mind for some time. I want to try to get a post as headmistress of a village school, something that would provide me with my own house or cottage.'

'You want to leave home?' Mrs Bray said in amazement.

'Yes, I do. After all, I'm nearly thirty and it is about time I became a little more independent. What do you think of the idea, Father?'

'You have done well at teaching,

Harriet, and I think you have earned your promotion. I think it is singularly forthcoming and independent of you to wish to advance in your career.'

His words were pompous but Harriet could have hugged her father for his support of her idea.

'Thank you, Father, I'm glad I have your approval. I would very much like to live in the country but transport is always a problem in rural areas. I want to buy a motor car.'

Her father looked at her gravely and her mother with astonishment. Harriet felt amused at their reactions and pressed her case.

'There are lots of ladies who drive in Waterbridge already,' she said. 'Just think of the advantages. I would be able to come home and see you and I could even take you out on a drive.'

This last remark did nothing to take the look of horror from Mrs Bray's face and once again it was left to Mr Bray to smoothe things over.

'I have been thinking of buying a

motor car myself but thought perhaps I was too old to learn such things. You have youth on your side, Harriet, but have you thought of the cost?'

'I have saved money during the war, Father, and I thought that if I looked for a second-hand model, I might be able to manage. But do you think, if I have not sufficient, you could lend me some money and I will repay it when I am earning more?'

Her father smiled for the first time, proud of his daughter.

'Of course I will, Harriet, and if you like, I will come to the Motor Company with you to help you choose one.'

Harriet gave him an unexpected hug.

'Can we go tomorrow, then?'

Twenty-four hours later, Harriet was the proud owner of a Ford Model T which dated from before the war but had been little used and was in good condition. Mr Farthing of the Motor Company had promised that one of his men would give her lessons the following week and that same day, Harriet wrote her letter to the Education Department asking for a move. She felt that indeed she was putting her plans into actions.

January came and went, a month of dreary, cold weather with little of the bright sunshine and sparkling white frost which can help the year into spring. For Harriet it was a month of trying not to think about Daniel and becoming immersed in schoolwork again. On the few fine weekends, she took delight in driving into the country and on one of those occasions she took John and Amy with her, much to the delight of both of them.

But for Amy, the high spot of the month was her visit to the Tottle home. John had invited her soon after Christmas and although she looked forward to the visit, she felt rather nervous. She made herself a new dress for the occasion with her grandmother's help. She had seen a dress in the leading draper's in the town, in the latest fashion, and she drew the design for Mrs Bartlett. They soon had it made up in a soft brown wool.

On the day she put the last stitch to it, she rushed round to the shop to show it to her mother and Mrs Bartlett. At the back of the shop she could hear a harsh coughing and when she went through to the kitchen, she found her mother bending over the sink, fighting for breath.

'Are you all right, Mother?' she asked gently.

Her mother straightened up and looked at Amy. Her face seemed thin and more lined but she managed a smile and gave Amy a kiss. Still gasping slightly, she went to the gas cooker.

'Yes, thank you, dear. I just came down to make your grandma a cup of tea and I started coughing. I'm all right now. Will you have a drink now that you are here?'

'Yes, please, Mother. I'll carry the tray up for you. I've come to show you something.'

'What's that then?'

'It's the new dress that Grandma has been helping me to make. I'm wearing it when I go to John's house this afternoon.'

They went upstairs to Mrs Bartlett's room where the dress was duly appraised and then admired. Amy spent an hour with them and as she left, she wondered just how much her mother was really coughing and not telling them about it. She knew that her father went in to see Dorrie every day, which had not been his previous custom and she wondered if he, too, sensed that Dorrie was not as well as she had been.

John called for Amy on the dot of two o'clock and together they walked out along the Taunton road. It was cold and cloudy but dry, a good day for a brisk winter walk.

By the end of the afternoon, Amy wondered why she had felt nervous. Mrs Tottle had made her feel so at home and Amy found that she was very fond and proud of her school-teacher husband and her son in the bank. It was a happy occasion and after tea, John and Amy walked back to Rhodes Place, silent and content. He pulled her into his arms and gave her a hug.

'Amy,' he whispered, 'it's been a lovely afternoon. Thank you.'

Her look was as loving as his and as their lips came together, they were both remembering the happiness of the afternoon and perhaps hoping that it had taken them nearer to the promise of a future together.

The wintry weather and her friendship with John continued but the first week in February brought Amy a problem. She had seen an announcement in the Waterbridge Mercury that a Victory Dance was to take place at the Town Hall at the end of the month. She longed to go for there would sure to be the usual waltzing and dancing competitions. She hadn't thought of Percy very much and she had to confess that she had hardly missed him, but now she was faced with what to do about the Victory Dance.

John did not dance, not even the waltz, he said, but how could she stay away, she asked herself. It would be the grandest occasion in Waterbridge of the whole year. If George had been home on leave she could have danced with him and she knew she would have to summon up courage to ask John if he would take her, even if he did not dance.

It took her the whole evening to summon that courage and it was as they were standing at the gate in Rhodes Place that she finally blurted out her request.

'John, I want to ask you something.'

John was getting to know Amy well, and that tone usually meant she was afraid he was going to say no. And how did he say no to her? His one aim in life was to please her.

'Not the motorcycle again, Amy!' he teased.

'No, John, it's not that. It's the Victory Dance.'

'The Victory Dance?' he said, sounding puzzled.

'Yes, it's at the Town Hall at the end of the month and I want to go. Everyone in Waterbridge will be there.'

John looked bemused.

'Well, that's all right. I'll take you.'

'You will take me? But you say you don't dance.'

'Well, that doesn't matter. We can sit and watch the dancing, can't we?'

'But, John, what if I want to dance? I usually go in for the waltzing competition.'

'Whom would you dance with, Amy?' he asked, frowning now.

'Oh, John, that's the trouble. There will be lots of young men there with whom I could dance but . . . '

She had been right to hesitate. John took her up immediately.

'But I wouldn't like you dancing with anyone else.'

'No, I didn't think you would,' she replied and then she continued.

'You see, I used to dance with Percy Venn. He wasn't my young man,' she hastened to add, 'but he is away in the army.'

John was silent for a moment before he continued.

'Amy, don't worry about it. I don't want to be a killjoy and I don't want to stop you dancing. Your happiness means too much to me. Let's wait until the night. I'll take you to the dance with pleasure then when we get there, we might even find a friend of mine who would do the waltz with you.'

The radiance of Amy's smile was reward enough for John. She reached up and kissed him on the lips in her gratitude.

'Thank you, John. You are a real sport.'

Amy was determined to make herself a new dance dress for the occasion. She had kept a length of cream lace for quite a long time and she knew that this was the time to use it. The sewing machine at Mrs Bartlett's whirred that week with Dorrie and Grandma Bartlett taking the keenest delight in the making of the dress.

On the night of the dance, Amy was dressed and ready early. Her father was nowhere to be seen and she assumed he had gone to see Dorrie. He had been rather quiet of late and she had no idea if he was going to put in an appearance at the dance.

Mrs Chidgey was all excitement and admiration and said she would open the door to John. He stood in the hall, looking handsome in his suit and best coat, and waited for Amy to come downstairs. She came at last and she knew she looked her best in the cream lace which showed up the deep burnished auburn of her hair to advantage.

She held out a hand to John and he took it in both of his.

'Amy, you look beautiful. The dress looks as though it came from one of the top fashion houses.'

Amy smiled in amusement but

secretly felt thrilled and flattered.

'Oh, John, as though I could afford a dress from one of the fashion houses! I'm glad you like it though.'

'Here are your coat and hat. Wrap up warm. It's a lovely night but cold.'

All through the town, couples were making their way to the Town Hall. There were a few carriages and one or two motor cars but most people were on foot, hurrying to be at this important social occasion. They crowded into the Town Hall and John took his and Amy's coats to the cloakroom. The main body of the hall, which was to be used for dancing, was decorated in red, white and blue and the stage, with ferns and draperies, was set apart for whist players and those who did not wish to dance.

John and Amy sat on one side watching a few couples who had already taken to the floor. Many people spoke to John and Amy was pleased to meet some of his acquaintances. His mother and father were there and in the distance, Amy could see Harriet sitting with Mr and Mrs Bray. It was such a colourful scene that for the time being, Amy was happy to sit and watch the dancers and to look at some of the dresses.

If John was sorry he did not dance, he did not show it and chatted quite happily. Amy caught Harriet's eye across the room and gave a little wave. Harriet immediately said something to her mother and got up and made her way around the crowded hall to the place where John and Amy were sitting. They were happily gossiping to one another when Amy felt the girl beside her go rigid.

Surprised, she looked at Harriet's face to see the colour drain from it, leaving her white and tense. She started to ask Harriet if she was not well when her eye caught sight of a small group of late arrivals. The tall, suited figure could only be that of her father. Amy half rose and then saw to her astonishment that he had a lady on his arm. It was Dorrie. She rose quickly and excitedly, forgetting Harriet, and half ran to meet her parents.

'Father, Mother, fancy you coming to the dance. Come and sit with us. John is there and Harriet, too.'

She was looking at her mother as she said the words but a stiffening in her father's figure caused her to look up at his face. It was tightly-controlled as though he was making a concentrated effort to conceal his emotions. Then, as he listened to Amy's voice, he relaxed and managed a half smile and they started to walk towards the seats that Amy had pointed out.

In the few minutes that Amy had darted forward, Harriet, rooted to her seat, tried to pull herself together. She knew that she should return to her parents but she could not move. She had prepared herself for this. At least, she had prepared herself to meet Daniel but Daniel accompanied by his wife she was totally unprepared for.

What she had expected Daniel's wife

to look like, Harriet did not know but she did know that the sight of the small, frail woman who walked slowly through the hall filled her with pity and a tremendous guilt. She looked up from the little figure to her tall partner and as she did so she met Daniel's eyes. They were imploring her to understand, to have mercy, to be kind. Harriet came to her senses at that look. She would not let him down and she stood up as the trio reached them. In a haze, she heard Daniel's voice.

'Harriet, good evening. I am pleased to find you here. And I would like to introduce you to my wife. Dorrie, this is Miss Harriet Bray. I think you will have heard Amy speak of her.'

Harriet shook hands with Dorrie and looked at the small, thin face. Amy is very like her even though she has her father's colouring, she was thinking. And then a soft voice spoke.

'Miss Bray, I think I will call you Harriet because that is what Amy calls you. I have heard all about your motor car and I must confess that I thought you were encouraging Amy in her tomboyish ideas but now I meet you, I can see that I can trust her with you.'

Harriet had no idea what she replied and was glad when Amy chipped in.

'Mother, are you sure you are well enough to be out in the cold? I never expected to see you here.'

Her mother smiled at her.

'I wouldn't have missed such a grand occasion, Amy, and Daniel very kindly hired a car and we were driven here.'

During this conversation, Daniel had been talking to John and had not glanced in Harriet's direction. He seemed to be relieved that one of the most difficult moments in his life was over. Harriet could see her parents looking in her direction and after talking for a little while to Amy and Dorrie, she said that she must rejoin her mother and father. She shook hands with Dorrie and was surprised at the sparkle in the fading eyes.

'I am very pleased to have met Amy's

friend and hope that Amy will bring you to see me one day,' Dorrie said quietly and sincerely.

Harriet made her farewells. As she reached her parents' side, her father looked at her.

'Harriet, you don't look well and your mother is suffering from the heat as well. Would you mind if I took you home now?'

They were the most welcome words she had ever heard and she gladly went to fetch the coats and hats. Coming out of the cloakroom, it was somehow not a shock to Harriet to bump into Daniel.

'Harriet, just one little minute. I must speak to you. Come behind these palms, please.'

7

In a daze, Harriet let herself be guided and found herself looking up at the beloved face, now so full of anguish and anxiety.

'Harriet, can you forgive me? I couldn't let you know. Dorrie didn't think of coming until tea-time. She wanted to come so much, I had to bring her.'

Somehow the sound of his voice had brought back a semblance of commonsense to her and she was able to reply quite coherently.

'Daniel, you don't have to apologise, not to me. I'm glad I've met Mrs Holley. I had quite a chat with her and she is very fond of Amy. I'm glad, Daniel, glad. Can you understand?'

'Harriet, my dear, what can I say?'

'You don't have to say any more. You know what I resolve to do and nothing will change it. I expect to hear from the Education Department any day now. I promise I won't go away without telling you. But I must go. Mother isn't well and they are waiting for the coats. Goodbye, Daniel.'

'Goodbye, Harriet.'

He went back to Dorrie and after a brief period, when they watched the dancing and had some supper, they, too, made their farewells.

Supper time had passed and still Amy had not danced. She was beginning to feel restive especially as she knew that the competition for the waltz would soon be announced and she had found no partner. John had been considerate and had asked one or two of his friends but they seemed no keener on dancing than John.

Her opportunity to dance when it came, was as sudden as it was unexpected. She felt a touch on her shoulder and, looking up, saw a young soldier standing there.

'Hello, Amy.'

She could not believe it — he looked so different.

'Percy!'

He not only looked taller but had put on weight which was especially noticeable around his face and neck. His complexion was reddened and contrasted markedly to his hair, still fair and curly.

'Percy, this is my friend, John Tottle. He works at the bank. John, this is Percy Venn.'

John stood up and Amy was instantly aware of the frigid atmosphere. The two young men shook hands and exchanged greetings but to Amy, the look that passed between them was nothing short of hostile. Percy did not help the situation by his next remark.

'Are you going to have a dance with me, Amy? The waltzing competition is coming up soon. Are you going in for it?'

'I'm not dancing tonight, Percy. John doesn't dance.'

The look that Percy gave John could

only be described as one of contempt. What was going on here, he wondered. Amy Holley sitting in silence with a young man he did not even like the look of and not even dancing! He would have to take a hand. He sat down at Amy's side and looked across at John.

'Would you mind if I partnered Amy in the competition? We used to win all the competitions in the old days. Would you like to, Amy?'

Amy couldn't breathe a word. She just did not know what to say but she looked up at John beseechingly. John was polite but very begrudging.

'I know that Amy is longing to go in for the competition. If you would like to enter together, I don't mind. I will watch.'

He felt his arm grabbed and Amy bubbled over in her gratitude and excitement. He knew he had pleased her but did not feel in the least happy about it as he looked at the young soldier at Amy's side.

In the ten minutes before the announcement of the competition, Percy did not stop talking and Amy was beginning to feel embarrassed. He didn't used to be like this, she thought, and she looked at his red face. Had he been drinking? She put the thoughts from her mind and tried to concentrate on the dancers, finally standing up with Percy for the waltz.

There was no doubt that they were a striking couple, Amy in her cream dress and her copper-coloured hair contrasting with Percy's uniform and his fair good looks. And they could waltz. Even John could not deny that and the jealousy of the previous ten minutes was replaced with a feeling of pride.

When it came to the last two couples, the judges had difficulty in deciding the winners. They changed the partners round and Amy danced with a tall, young man she did not know but with whom she waltzed perfectly and they were proclaimed the winners amid great applause.

Amy collected her prize, a small silver trophy, and hastened back towards John, not noticing that Percy was approaching her, not too pleased.

As Percy reached her, he drew her into a dim alcove. His hand felt forceful and she did not like the feeling of coercion.

'Percy, let me go. I'm sorry you did not win but thank you for dancing with me. I want to go now and show my trophy to John.'

'John, is it, now? I suppose Percy isn't good enough for you any more.'

She tried to pull away from him but he did not release her and his flushed face came nearer hers. Still she tried to get away but he pulled her farther into the alcove and pinned her against the wall, his mouth descending on hers in a sudden, savage kiss.

As suddenly as she was made prisoner of the frustrated, young soldier, Amy was free. She opened her terrified eyes to see John towering over Percy, hitting out at him with fierce blows.

'Stop it, stop it,' Amy cried out in agitation, her voice distraught.

She was still clutching her trophy and she threw it at them as though she hoped that the futile gesture would stop the brawling men. Sobbing, she pummelled John on the back. But her protestations were useless and she found herself screaming out even as they fought.

'I'm not staying and I don't ever want to see you again, John Tottle, or you, Percy Venn.'

She scrambled away from them and as she made her escape she heard the still angry John called out.

'I don't want a girl who kisses her old boy-friend the minute he turns up.'

Amy didn't pause. Tears streaming down her face, she found her coat and hat and left the building and the horrible scene behind her. She ran as fast as she could until she arrived at the gate of her home, panting and still gulping sobs. Rushing up the path, she almost collided with her father who was unlocking the front door.

'Amy,' he said in astonishment as he saw the state she was in.

She burst into tears once again as he gathered her up and half carried her into the house.

'Whatever has happened? Why are you on your own and where's John?'

The name produced fresh floods of tears and he sat her on the sofa in the sitting-room, kneeling beside her, hardly knowing what to do to calm the distraught girl.

'Sit there, Amy! Don't move. I'll go and get you a cup of tea.'

He hurried off and by the time he was back, he was relieved to find that she was calmer and giving little hiccups and half-sobs as she tried to put her hair in order.

'Drink this,' he said, holding out the cup and she took it gratefully.

'Have you quarrelled with John?' he asked after several moments.

'It's worse than that, Dad. There was a terrible scene. You will be ashamed of me. I'm sorry, Dad, I really am.'

'Amy, are you going to tell me what happened? You don't have to but it would help if I knew what had upset you so much.'

She looked at his kind, familiar face and told him the story. She left nothing out. Then as she finished, a glimmer of humour returned to her and she gave him a tiny smile.

'And I threw the trophy at them so I haven't even got that.'

But her father was still serious.

'I think that's the least of your worries, my dear. I am very sorry about John. I like John very much and I had hoped . . . '

But he wasn't allowed to finish for Amy was beginning to feel angry.

'Don't mention him,' she said. 'If he's going to get as jealous as that just because I danced with Percy Venn and then start a fight before I could explain things, well, I just don't want to know him. In fact, I'm forgetting about young men altogether. I've just decided.'

A gleam came into her eye.

'I will get Grandma to write to her friend in Bristol and I'll go away and train to be a milliner. You wouldn't mind, would you, Dad?'

'They say the path of true love never runs smoothly, Amy, and I think it's true,' Daniel said seriously.

He spoke with such feeling she looked at him curiously. Some hidden emotion lay in his eyes but she caught only a fleeting glimpse of it. He suddenly put out his arms and caught her in a fond hug.

'I would miss you, Amy, but you must do what you think is right.'

The following day, Amy asked Grandma Bartlett to write to her friend with the milliner's shop in Bristol and for the rest of the week waited anxiously for a reply. She tried not to think of John and dreaded the day when she would have to see him at the bank.

In the end, it worked out that both events happened on the same day. When Amy arrived at the shop, Dorrie had opened up. She looked tired but she was obviously excited about something.

'Amy, your grandma has heard from her friend in Bristol. Run upstairs quickly and find out what she's got to say. I'll look after the shop for you.'

Amy gave her mother a quick kiss and ran up the stairs.

'You've heard, Grandma! What does she say? Will she have me?'

Mrs Bartlett smiled.

'Calm down, Amy. I'm not sure if you're going to like it. Mildred says that she would love to have you if I think you have a talent for millinery but she hasn't got a vacancy at the moment. But as a favour to me, she would be willing to take you on as an apprentice for two months and she would teach you all she could in that time.'

137

Mrs Bartlett looked at her grand-daughter keenly and she saw excitement light up the young face.

'That's good news, Amy, but I'm afraid there's a big snag.'

'What do you mean?'

'We would have to find the money for the apprenticeship.'

'How much?' Amy asked in dis-appointment.

'It's fifty pounds but that would include your board and lodging. She has a room she could offer you above the shop.'

'Oh, it's a lot of money, Grandma.'

Amy faltered then her expression changed as she had a sudden thought.

'But I've got some money saved up. It was for something special I haven't told you about. Dad knows and maybe if I give up that idea then perhaps he would lend me some money. I'll run straight home and ask him, if Mum wouldn't mind staying in the shop for a while. Is she all right, Grandma?'

'She's not well, Amy, not well at all.

It's her chest but she's a good daughter to me and I don't know how I would have managed without her being here. Now off you go and see what Daniel has to say, then I can write back to Mildred.'

Amy ran nearly all the way back to Rhodes Place and just caught her father before he went out collecting his rent. He had bought himself a motor-car but said that it was too ostentatious to go round to his tenants in a car. He still preferred the pony and trap.

'Dad,' Amy called, out of breath. 'Wait a minute, I've got something to ask you.'

She told him the news and he listened to her seriously.

'It's a lot of money, Amy, and I've just bought the motor-car.'

She caught hold of his arm.

'I'll use my savings,' she told him. 'You know I've been saving up for a motor-cycle.'

He gave a shout of laughter.

'Do you mean you would rather be a

milliner than ride a motor-cycle, Amy? You are a funny girl.'

'I'm not,' she almost stamped her foot but she knew he was teasing her. 'I've nearly got enough if you could possibly lend me the rest.'

'Amy, I'll give you the whole lot of it means we can make a milliner of you and then when your apprenticeship is finished, we'll look round for a shop for you. How about that?'

'You are a father in a million,' she said. 'I love you.'

That afternoon, Amy felt awkward as she went into the bank. John was busy with another customer and she had to wait her turn. Then their eyes met and the look in John's gave Amy courage.

'John, I've got something to tell you. Could you come round tonight?' she whispered.

'Yes, all right. I'll come at seven o'clock.'

When the time came for John's visit, Amy heard her father letting him in. She ran down the stairs but hesitated as she reached the bottom. At the same time, John turned towards her and simply held out his arms. He was smiling and she went to him. He held her close as though he never wanted to let her go.

'I'm glad you could come, John,' she said.

He touched her forehead with his lips and said gently, 'I've come to say I'm sorry, Amy. I have regretted my behaviour ever since that night at the Town Hall and every minute of the day I have longed to see you and tell you how I felt. I just couldn't have kept away any longer. If you hadn't have come to the bank this afternoon, I still would have come.'

'Oh, John, I've wanted to see you so much, too, but I thought I really was in disgrace. Shall we go for a walk?'

They strolled slowly in the soft evening air, John's arm around Amy's shoulders.

'Why did you ask me to come, Amy?'

'I've got some news for you. I don't know if you'll be pleased or not, but I wouldn't like you to be cross again. I couldn't bear that.'

'Amy, I honestly will try not to be cross with you again. I'm so ashamed of making such a scene but I just saw red when I could see that Percy was kissing you.'

She looked up at him.

'John, it was my fault as well. I shouldn't have insisted on dancing. I'm sorry, but I hope you will believe me when I tell you that I didn't realise that Percy was going to kiss me. He was quite rough and I was trying to get away from him. I think he had been drinking. You came and hit him before I had a chance to explain and I lost my temper, too. I'm really sorry it all happened as it did.'

They started to laugh.

'I'm glad you've come. I've got such a lot to tell you. Do you know Bristol, John?'

'Yes, it's very nice. My brother lives

there. As a matter of fact, we're hiring a car on Sunday and I'm taking Mother and Father to see the family so I'm afraid I won't be able to see you, Amy. But that's enough about Bristol. What is your news? I'm dying to hear it.'

'Well, it's about Bristol really.'

His face fell as he looked at her.

'Oh, Amy, not the hat shop again?'

John knew what she had been planning and had hoped she had forgotten the idea. Then she told him about the letter they had received and she talked so quickly and excitedly that John couldn't help being caught up in the wave of enthusiasm.

'And it's only for two months,' he said at last.

'Yes,' she replied, 'and I can live above the shop so I will be quite safe. And another thing. I'm going to use my savings for my motor-cycle for the apprenticeship money.'

'You mean you won't be buying a motor-cycle after all?'

She nodded.

'Yes. I can't do both.'

'Well, that's something but, Amy, I've no need to tell you that I don't want you to go away. We've had our ups and downs and we really are becoming good friends, aren't we?'

Amy waited. His opinion was so important to her. She wanted to go to Bristol but she also wanted John Tottle and she knew that if he disapproved then she would have to forget the whole idea. Then came his verdict.

'I do believe that it is sensible for a girl to be trained for something. I know that I disagreed about the motor-cycle but that was because of the safety as much as anything. Amy, I know I will miss you but it's only for two months and I do think it would be foolish not to take it up.'

He was allowed to say no more. Her arms were around his neck and he picked her up and swung her off her feet.

'Oh, John, thank you, thank you. I wouldn't have gone if you'd said no but I'm so pleased and thankful that you approve.'

'You wouldn't have gone if I'd said no?'

Amy realised that she had given herself away and it was in a small voice that she said, 'No, I wouldn't.'

He gave her a quick kiss.

'Then it is I who should be saying thank you. And Amy, I've got something for you.'

'What is it?' she asked as she saw him put his hand in his pocket and pull out something silver and shining.

She smiled with delight.

'Oh, it's my trophy, John. Did you find it for me?'

'Yes. When Percy had gone, I looked for it. I was ashamed, Amy. I didn't know I could be so jealous.'

He was smiling as he pulled her close to him. As they walked home, they made plans and John said that after her first month in Bristol, he might have a car and would come and visit her.

The next morning was a Saturday

and Amy was surprised by a visit from Harriet in the shop, quite early in the morning. Harriet seemed not to be her usual calm self but somehow excited and disturbed. Amy was soon to find out why.

'Amy, I did want to see you. I hope your mother is well. I've got so much to do and such a lot of news! It's all happened at once.'

'I've got some news for you, too, but please let me hear yours first.'

'It only happened yesterday afternoon. Mr Stradling, the headmaster, had a visit from someone from County Hall. They wanted him to spare one of his teachers as a matter of urgency to go to Nether Pound, a village near llminster. I told you I was trying for a headship, didn't I? Well, it's turned out that the headmistress at Nether Pound was due to retire next term but she has broken her leg and is in hospital.

'They need someone straight away as the infant teacher is trying to manage on her own. They have asked me if

146

I would like to go there. Isn't it wonderful? Oh, and there's a small house attached to the school that I can have, so I am busy getting all my things together.'

'I'm very pleased, Harriet, and you've got your car, too. It couldn't have worked out better. When do you start?'

'On Monday. I've hardly time to turn round. Oh, and Father sent this letter for Mr Holley. Can you give it to him today? I think it's quite urgent.'

Amy noticed the trembling hand as Harriet gave her the white envelope. Something other than the move to the school was upsetting Harriet. Amy was sure of it, but she soon forgot as she told Harriet of her own plans.

'Well done, Amy. We must write to each other. When you have your address, write to me at the School House, Nether Pound. I must go, Amy. There is so much to see to.'

Amy watched Harriet hurry up Eastfield, pleased for her friend yet sensing an air of something unexplained.

8

As Harriet hurried up Eastfield, her mind was not on Amy, not on her move to her new school but on Daniel. In fact, her thoughts had never been far from Daniel since her meeting with him at the Victory Dance when she had met him with Dorrie. After the shock of the meeting, Harriet had gone home, knowing that it was right that she had met Dorrie for it had left her more determined than ever to move away.

Daniel might have no real love left for his wife but he was caring for her in her illness and that alone evoked admiration for him in Harriet. If Dorrie had been unpleasant or critical, domineering or unloving, Harriet would have fought for Daniel's love but she could never put up a fight against such a woman. As she walked home now, her mind was in chaos. She could not go away from Daniel for ever without saying goodbye to him, indeed she had promised him. She longed to see him just once more and the envelope she had given to Amy for him was a brief note to explain about the move and to ask if she could see him just for a few minutes to say goodbye. She knew it was wrong yet she had no sense of wrong-doing.

On the Sunday afternoon of the following week-end, at the same time as Harriet was getting ready for her meeting with Daniel, Amy had decided to go for a walk along the river. It was a fine afternoon and John had gone to Bristol. She strolled along the river path and when she passed a small wood, she remembered from her childhood that it was there they had always admired the first primroses. She had to search for them in the trees but when she found them, she had not the heart to pick the beautiful flowers. It's like finding gold, she thought.

As she came out of the trees, the

sunlight dazzled her and she stopped where she was when she saw someone walking rather hurriedly along the river bank in the direction of the railway bridge. There was a familiarity in the person's movement that made Amy stay hidden among the trees.

She looked again, unsure, puzzled and then, as she saw the face of the walker, she was certain. It was Harriet! Something made her stop herself from calling out. Harriet did not give the impression that she was out for a Sunday stroll. She strode along purposefully without turning her head. Suddenly she pulled the hood of her cloak over her head.

Amy, with her fertile imagination, thought it must be that Harriet was meeting someone in secret. And Amy, feeling embarrassed, decided to stay where she was for a moment before slipping from the wood and making her way back across the fields. It was that moment of hesitation that brought Amy the revelation that shattered her world.

She could still see the hooded figure of Harriet walking quickly towards a group of trees by the bridge where from the cover of the trees a tall person advanced and held out his arms. Amy was transfixed. She knew the man, recognised him. It was her father!

Amy watched motionless as Harriet started to run towards him. As she tripped slightly, she was snatched safely into his arms then drawn back into the shelter of the tall trees. Amy moved at last. She turned and ran back into the wood, in her panic scratching herself on the bare branches. At last she flung herself into the moss and flowers. She lay there stiff, unbelieving, frozen by the appalling truth of the scene she had just witnessed.

Amy cried out loud, a long-drawn-out moan. Then she was stilled by a flood of memories, of impressions which told her the truth. There was the startling reaction from both Harriet and Daniel when she had first introduced

151

them in the shop. She remembered clearly the looks on their faces.

She remembered them, too, on Fair Day and then how eager her father had been to take Harriet home on Armistice Day. And the most recent occurrence, only yesterday morning when Harriet gave her the letter from Mr Bray to her father. Amy now knew the truth of the letter. It must have been a note from Harriet herself to arrange this very meeting. Harriet was going away tomorrow and would want to say a farewell.

Questions which she could not answer surged through her teeming brain. What was there between the two? Did they love each other? Was Harriet going away because of her love? Then there was her mother. Her father had been so much kinder to Dorrie of late and Amy wondered now if he had felt guilty because of his love for Harriet.

Suddenly, Amy understood the tragedy of their love, the agony they must have gone through. This scene by the river had been the very end. Harriet would go away and her father would continue to care for poor Dorrie.

She left the wood then and made her decision. She would tell no-one, not even John. Their secret would be her secret. She loved both of them. What she had just seen and what she now knew, she must hide from the world and above all from her dear father and mother.

Back by the river, Daniel had found a small, shaded copse among the tangled undergrowth, where a tree was lying, dead. They sat together, his arms around Harriet.

'You were worried, my dear one,' he whispered.

'Oh, Daniel, I seem to have so many fears and worries and I can't believe that I am safely here. Daniel, it is the last time I shall see you. I am going away tomorrow.'

'Tell me all about it so that I can always picture you. We are going to

153

be sensible and not sorrowful. Tell me what you know about Nether Pound, about the school and where you will be living.'

Harriet put her hand in his and told him what she knew about the village and the school and he listened to every word. Then there was something she knew she must ask him.

'Daniel, I have to ask you. I know you have a motor car now but you wouldn't come and visit me, would you?'

'Harriet, always know that I will respect your wishes. I know you are right. No, I wouldn't seek you out. You are quite safe and you must have peace of mind and freedom to start a new life.'

She squeezed his hand.

'Thank you. I was sure that you would understand and you do. For the same reason, I cannot write to you and you must not write to me.'

Daniel lifted her hand to his lips.

'It's strange, Harriet. We have only

been on our own three or four times but I feel that I have known you for a life-time, just as though you have always been there and will always be part of my life. Can you begin to understand?'

'Yes, I do understand for I feel the same myself. That is true love, isn't it, Daniel?'

'That is love, Harriet. I shall never stop loving you however long we are separated.'

'Daniel, I don't want all your love. I want you to save some for Dorrie, Amy and your family. They need you.'

'I know, my dear, and I promise you that I will never let them down. It's a promise that I made in marriage and I will not break it. Before I met you, my marriage was already breaking up. I was bad-tempered and had become impatient with Dorrie. Now I seem to be able to try harder somehow. I think you have made me more understanding and caring.'

Harriet stood up then and put her

hand into Daniel's. She could feel his strength and it passed on to her the strength to say the last words.

'Goodbye, Daniel. I must go now.'

He gripped her hand until it hurt.

'Goodbye, my Harriet, and always remember that I love you.'

She stumbled away from him on the uneven ground and did not look back as she ran out of the copse. She prayed for the strength to face the world on her own, without Daniel, without his love.

On the Monday morning that Harriet was to leave for Nether Pound, Amy was awake early. She lay thinking of the two who were uppermost in her mind since the scene along the river the previous afternoon. She had dreaded meeting her father but when she reached home, the motor car was missing. He returned home late, and she guessed that he had taken himself off to walk alone somewhere quiet.

Now, it was Harriet she was thinking of and she made up her mind to go and see her friend off so that her last impression of Harriet was not that of a solitary walk followed by a forbidden embrace. All was activity at Regent's Square but Amy helped to pack a few things into the tiny car and stood with Mr and Mrs Bray to wave Harriet off. Amy then went back to the shop with some feeling of relief and a determination to treat the disturbing incident as completely over.

Two days later, all these worries were banished from Amy's mind by a letter from Mildred Evans saying that she would be pleased if Amy could start the following week. They were in the run-up to Easter and would welcome extra help in the work-room. Amy could have two days off to go home at Easter and then return to Bristol for a further month afterwards.

That week, Amy saw John every evening and when Sunday came, he carried her carefully-packed case to the station for her. Amy was inclined to be tearful as she said goodbye to him but as soon as the train pulled out of the station, her sense of excitement returned.

MADAME MILDRED, MILLINER was a small, exclusive shop in a street just off Park Street in a fashionable part of Bristol. Amy found it easily and was given a kind welcome by Madame Mildred herself. She was taken to her room and then shown the shop and the work-room.

After that, the time flew past in a whirl of hard work in the work-room which matched up to Amy's wildest dreams. It was full to overflowing with felt, and feathers and plumes, artificial flowers and bunches of fruit, everything a milliner would need in making a hat. Amy learned quickly and Madame Mildred was pleased with her.

Amy soon made a good friend of Hetty who worked in the shop and proved to be a great help to her. She had little time to think of her father and Harriet but letters from John came every other day and she usually spent her evenings writing to him. She also wrote to Harriet with her new address and was pleased to receive a reply by return post.

Dear Amy,

I was very pleased to receive your address as I have been wondering how you were getting on. Thank you for writing to me. Your life sounds quite hectic but I am glad that you are enjoying it. Life is quite busy here, too, as I teach all ages in the junior school instead of just a class of one age as I did at Eastfields.

There is a very nice girl who teaches the infants and we are good friends and often go out together in my car which, I must tell you, is a seven-day wonder in Nether Pound! The only other car in the village belongs to the doctor.

I think my greatest delight is my little house. It is built on to the school and there is a very nice elderly couple living next door. Mr Rowsell is the caretaker and sees to the stoves in the school and spoils me by seeing to my range for me.

I have discovered that an old school friend of mine lives nearby. Lilian is married to Joe Frost and he has a nursery for plants and trees and things. They have three small children and they make me very welcome on Sundays when I usually go to see them.

So as you can see, I am contented with my move and I am sure I made the right decision. Life has changed for both of us.

With love, Harriet.

Amy put down the letter. Reading between the lines, there seemed to be no hint of sadness or regret and Amy was pleased.

In no time at all, Amy found herself back in the train to go home to Waterbridge at Easter. When she stepped on to the platform at the railway station, John was there to meet her. She ran straight into his arms.

'Oh, John,' she cried out as he kissed her. 'It seems such a long time since I saw you. Have you missed me?'

'I have,' he replied as he picked up her case. 'I couldn't wait for you to come home. I've got a surprise for you.'

She walked by his side out to the station forecourt. She guessed the surprise was Harriet, for standing there was Harriet's car.

'Is Harriet home as well?' she asked.

'No, it's not Harriet. This is my motor car. It's the same model as Harriet's but a year or two older. Do you like it?'

Amy walked round the little car then reached up and gave John a kiss.

'It's a lovely surprise and I think it's beautiful.'

'Will you come out with me this afternoon, Amy?'

'Yes, I'd love to as soon as I've been home and had time to go and see Mother and Grandma Bartlett.'

'I believe your mother's not very

well, Amy. I'd better prepare you. I saw your father and he said she'd had influenza badly. He's been spending a lot of time at the shop, and they've got a new girl behind the counter. She's called Ivy and she seems very nice. I think she's a cousin of that Percy Venn of yours.'

Amy sat beside him the car and listened to all the news and they were soon in Rhodes Place. John left her, promising to be back at two o'clock. Her father wasn't there but Mrs Chidgey was pleased to see her.

'I'm glad they've let you come home for Easter, Miss Amy. Your father is round at the shop. He's been there every day since your mother took ill.'

'I'll run round straight away, Mrs Chidgey. Why didn't they tell me?'

'Well, it started off as just influenza but it's gone to her chest. Coughing something dreadful, she's been. She'll be pleased to see you, Miss Amy.'

Amy hurried round to the shop and ran up the stairs to her mother's room.

When she saw the small, still figure, she thought she was too late. Then she realised that her father was sitting at the end of the bed and that he was reading the newspaper. He got up and hugged her.

'Oh, Amy, I'm so glad you have been able to come home,' he said.

'But Mother?'

'She's a little better today and she's having a peaceful sleep for once. Go and see Grandma until Dorrie wakes up.'

Amy did as he said and when Dorrie woke up, she was weak but cheerful, very pleased to see Amy and to hear all the news about the hat shop. Amy left her feeling happier and promised to go back with John later in the day. After lunch, John arrived and announced that he was going to take Amy up Holcombe Hill. Amy stared at him wide-eyed.

'Holcombe Hill? But, John, it is so long and steep. What about your car?'

He laughed.

'I want to try it out,' he told her. 'If it can cope with Holcombe Hill then I can go anywhere.'

Holcombe Hill was indeed a long hill but not all that steep. John's car took it easily, to John's delight. The April day was warm enough for Amy to be without a coat and she walked through the trees at the top of the hill, her hand in John's. She felt very contented. They stopped by a field gate where there was a fine view towards Waterbridge. Beyond, they could see the blue-grey sweep of the bay that was the Bristol Channel.

John was quiet and when she looked up at him, she saw that he was looking very serious. She was sure he had something on his mind. John had only one thing on his mind and that was Amy. He had known for a long time that he loved her but his cautious nature didn't let him rush into anything. Now, as he looked at the sweet, happy face, he knew he had chosen the right moment to speak.

'I've got something for you in my pocket, Amy, but I have something to say to you first. Amy, I love you. Will you marry me?'

He looked into her eyes and knew the answer even though she had not spoken, but he wanted to hear her reply.

'Amy, it will be some time before I am in a position to marry but that wouldn't stop us becoming engaged, would it? Please tell me you love me.'

Amy knew that there was only one answer.

'I do love you, John, and I will marry you if you would like me to.'

She was crushed in his arms in a passionate embrace. Amy knew that this was where she wanted to be for the rest of her life. John spoke at last.

'Amy, I was sure that you would say yes. I really was certain so I brought the ring with me.'

Amy was stuck for words in her delight and her amazement. They opened the box together and inside

Amy found a beautiful ring, a small single diamond set in gold.

'John, it is beautiful. Oh, I love it.'

'Are you sure, Amy? I felt it was the right one but we can change it if you don't like it.'

'I wouldn't change it for the world,' she said happily.

He slipped it on her engagement finger and they both stood staring down at the token of their love, of their future together. The ring was a perfect fit.

He drove back to Waterbridge where they called at the Tottles who were delighted with their news. Then they went on to the shop. Amy hoped that she wasn't going to upset her mother but Dorrie was sitting up in bed and smiled as they went into the room.

'Have you got some news for me?' she asked them but was overcome with a fit of coughing.

Amy held her mother's hand and when the coughing stopped and Dorrie was leaning back against the pillows exhausted, John came forward and they stood together as Amy whispered softly.

'John has asked me to marry him and I've said yes. He's given me an engagement ring, Mother.'

'Let me see it,' Dorrie said hoarsely.

Amy held out her hand and Dorrie smiled at them both.

'Nothing could have pleased me more. I always thought that John was the right one for you, Amy. I hope you'll both be very happy.'

Daniel came in then and there were more congratulations until he said that he wanted Dorrie to have another sleep. Amy and John left, Amy marvelling at the care her father was giving to Dorrie.

The newly-engaged couple had one more day together before John put Amy on the train back to Bristol where she would start the last few weeks of her apprenticeship. One of the first things she did on reaching Bristol was to write to Harriet to tell her the news. She received a long and friendly letter of congratulations in return.

Into her second week at the hat shop, Amy was busy on a summery hat in the work-room when Mrs Evans came in looking rather serious.

'Amy, there is someone to see you. He says his name is John Tottle and that he is your fiancé. I have put him in the drawing-room.'

Amy was both flustered and dismayed. Why should John come to Bristol in the middle of the week? She felt with a sinking of her heart that it could only be bad news. She hurried to Mrs Evans' drawing-room and ran straight into John's arms. He held her tight.

'Oh, Amy, I said I would come but I don't know how to tell you. I'm afraid your mother died in the night, Amy.'

'Mother?' Amy cried out. 'But she was getting better! Oh, John!'

'Your father came to the bank first thing this morning. He said that her breathing had been getting worse yesterday and she died peacefully in her sleep. He asked me if I would come and tell you and take you home. He needs you, Amy. He is very upset.'

Amy dried her tears.

'Yes, I must come. I will ask Mrs Evans. You stay here, John.'

Mrs Evans was kindness itself and said that Amy had done so well and had been such a help to her, that she would give her half the apprenticeship money back and that Amy needn't return. She would be needed at home.

John and Amy were silent all the way back to Waterbridge, Amy had so much to think about. At Rhodes Place, she was to find a very solemn household and after talking to her father, she went to see Grandma Bartlett. The old lady was sitting by the fire as though she had been waiting for the visit. Amy put her arms round her and kissed her.

'There, my dear,' Grandma Bartlett said. 'Dorrie was your mother and my daughter and we shall miss her but we must thank God that she is suffering no longer. It's Daniel we've got to think of. You go back to him and see what you can do to comfort him. I know that all was not well between them these last few years. I heard the quarrels the same as you did, but he was good to her in her illness and he has always been good to me, too.'

'But what about you, Grandma?'

'You're not to worry about me. I've got Ivy. She's a good girl and says she'll leave home and come and live here. It's all settled.'

From then on, Mrs Chidgey took charge, with calmness and with sensibility. She saw to everything, leaving Amy to try to comfort her father who, until after the funeral, seemed to live in a world of private grief and a guilt which he alone knew of.

9

A month went by and Amy became more and more worried about her father. She was at a loss, not really needed at the shop, and was filling in her time by helping Mrs Chidgey. She had written to Harriet to tell her about Dorrie and had received only a polite note in return.

Amy tried to spend as many evenings as possible with her father but there was John to consider. He had been very understanding. Late one evening, when she had been out for a walk with him, she returned to find her father sitting in his usual chair in the drawing-room. She went to him and kneeled by his side. He clutched his young daughter to him, overtaken suddenly by tears and grief.

'Amy, Amy, I am the most wicked man alive.'

Amy waited for him to speak again. When his words finally came, they were a torrent of confused time, people and emotions.

'I didn't mean to love her but she was so beautiful,' he said. 'And Dorrie had been so difficult, always complaining. How was I to know then that she was so ill? I had no patience, no patience at all. When we were younger it was different. She was pretty and we loved one another but she changed. She wasn't sweet, little Dorrie any more and I was left out. Her mother became more important to her. But if I had known she was so ill, I wouldn't have shouted at her. I would have tried harder. And now she has gone and I deceived her. I have the guilt of her death on my mind day and night. How can I go to her with this guilt on my hands? And I love her, I love her, Amy.'

To anyone but Amy this tirade of words would have been sheer nonsense, but her knowledge of her father's secret love gave her a clear insight into the torment that was going on in his mind. She took his hands in hers and looked earnestly into the sorrowful face.

'I know, Dad. I know.'

Her clear tones, her ring of sincerity and understanding seemed to pierce the blackness of his mood.

'What do you mean, Amy? What do you know? What have I told you?'

'I know about you and Harriet.'

'How can you know about Harriet? No-one knows. It is all between Harriet and myself and it is finished.'

Amy told him about that afternoon by the river, in the trees and how she had seen them together. He looked dumbfounded, but for the first time in four weeks, it focused his attention on something other than his own grief.

'Amy, what have I put you through?'

'As it turned out it was the best thing that could have happened because it means that I can talk to you. Perhaps I can even help you.'

'My dear Amy, it has helped me just to be able to talk to you. But tell me, how can I ever think of that fine girl and consider a future together?'

'Dad, you are being morbid. You have spent all these weeks looking on the black side of everything. You have even thought of yourself as wicked. But you are not. Look how good you are to me and to the boys and Grandma and look how you cared for Mother when she was ill. What have you done that is wrong? You have loved but your love did no wrong.'

'Whatever are you saying, Amy?'

'Think about it. You love Harriet but did you leave your family and go off with her? No, you did not. And what about Harriet? Did she try to lure you away from your family? No, she did not. It was Harriet who went away. She is a wonderful person and I love her, too, and it may not be the right time now but one day you will have each other. I know you will.'

Daniel's face had lightened, but Amy had not finished.

'Dad, it wouldn't be right if you

didn't grieve for Mother but it's not going to go on for ever and she wouldn't have wished it to. One day you'll go to Harriet and tell her you love her and want to marry her.'

'Amy!'

'In the meantime,' she continued, 'you are going to stop brooding about things and get yourself well again.'

'Amy,' he cried out. 'What would I do without you to keep me in order? Have you go something lined up to rejuvenate me?'

'Yes, I have. You can think of me for a start. I can't go back to the sweet shop. Ivy loves it there and Grandma needs her. I want something to do.'

'The hat shop?'

'Yes, the hat shop! Grandma and I have made quite a lot of models and soon I shall want a shop. So, Dad, dear, you start looking.'

'I promise you that I will shake myself out of this lethargy and see what I can do for you. Have you finished organising me yet?'

'Not quite,' she said and grinned at him. 'I want you to start going out for walks, get some fresh air and exercise. You have been indoors far too long.'

'I would do anything to please you, Amy, so I will say yes.'

Things happened quickly after that. Daniel threw off his lethargy and Amy cleared one of the attics at Rhodes Place and set about making hats. She even got John to take her to Bristol on a day trip and came back in a car laden with all the materials a milliner could possibly need.

She was in her room working one morning when her father came running up the stairs. He picked her up and whirled her round.

'Dad, Dad, put me down! Whatever is it?'

'I've found a shop!'

'You haven't,' Amy cried out. 'Where is it?'

'In the High Street! Couldn't be a better position.'

'They are all big shops there. I only

176

want a little place.'

'It's just off the High Street really, that little street opposite the church.'

Amy looked delighted.

'That's an ideal position. Just think, oh, dear, it's rather irreverent!' She grinned. 'But the people who go to church always wear smart hats and they would be able to look in the shop window on the way home.'

'The owner died last week and it's up for sale. It needs a lot doing to it so it's going quite reasonably. I think it would be a good investment, Amy.'

For Amy, the next few weeks became a whirl of activity. The purchase of the shop went forward and a transformation took place in that small establishment in just a few days. John was roped in and fortunately they were able to work well into the long, light summer evenings.

Amy was banished from the shop and told to stay at home and make hats. The next time she made a visit, she found that deep drawers and cabinets had been fitted, a work-room provided at the back and separated from the shop by a curtain of beads and it was ready for stocking up. A week later, the shop was ready to be opened. The great day had arrived!

It was a success from the start. On the opening morning, there was no mad rush but a steady stream of ladies who seemed delighted that the town had at last got a milliner. Most of them bought something or promised to come and buy a hat next time they needed one.

After that, Amy never had a spare moment. First thing in the morning was quiet and she devoted this time to making new hats, then the afternoon would be busy. John usually popped in to see her in his lunch hour when she closed the shop and they ate their sandwiches together. Amy felt that only one thing marred her happiness.

During the days of buying and preparing to open the shop, her father had thrown off his melancholy and she hoped that she had succeeded in shaking him out of his doubts and torments. But at mealtimes and in the evenings, he was often silent and morose. Although she was so busy herself, she knew that she must spend some time with him.

One Sunday evening, after she had been out with John, she found her father standing in the drawing-room in front of his china cabinet. His thoughts were far away and as Amy watched him, she knew he was thinking of Harriet. He turned, and as she had thought, his look was full of sorrow.

It's time to be bold again, Amy was saying to herself. Out loud she asked him a question.

'Have you written to Harriet, Dad?'

'Written to Harriet? How could I? What have I to say to her?'

He shot the questions at her irritably and Amy sighed. It was going to be more difficult than she had imagined.

'It is two months since Mother died and Harriet will have been thinking of you. I'm sure she would like to have some news.'

She swallowed hard.

'Has she a place in your life, Dad? If there is to be one then it is only fair to let her know where she stands.'

Shaken out of his apathy, Daniel looked at Amy with a hostile expression which startled her and made her heart sink.

'And what do you know about it, Amy? You're young, not yet twenty. What do you know about being too old to offer your life to someone like . . .'

He could not even say her name. But Amy stuck to her guns.

'You are not old, Dad. I know that you are my father but that's nothing to do with it. It's Harriet we've got to think of. You are some years older than Harriet, but that is nothing. John is five years older than me. What is age? It is love that matters in the end.'

'It cannot be, Amy. I shouldn't have shouted at you. You were only trying to help me, I know, but how can I offer myself to Harriet? She may reject me, and for all I know, she may have met someone younger. I love her still, but I can't do it!'

At his heartfelt cry, Amy left him. Her cheeks wet, she ran up to her room. She knew she had failed and she sat and thought for a long time. Finally, it was Harriet's face she could see most clearly. She had not succeeded with her father but what if she spoke to Harriet?

She would get John to take her to Nether Pound and she would talk to Harriet. What did it matter if she, Amy, knew of the love between her father and her friend? Certain that this love was true and lasting, she was going to do what she could to bring them together.

The following weekend, she asked John if they could go to visit Harriet and he seemed pleased at the idea. On the way there, Amy explained to him that she wanted to ask Harriet something of a private nature and would he mind having a walk round the village while she chatted to Harriet.

Harriet welcomed them gladly and they sat in the front room of the little cottage, talking mostly about Amy's shop. In a pause in the conversation, John got up.

'If you two girls don't mind,' he said, 'I think I'll leave you to it and have a stroll round the village. I haven't been here before.'

As soon as John had gone, Amy plunged straight in to what she had come to say.

'I want to talk to you about Dad, Harriet.'

'Amy, what do you mean? What are you talking about?'

Amy had to use the same candour that she had used with her father and hoped for more success this time.

'I know that you love each other, Harriet.'

'Amy!'

'No, Dad didn't tell me. Please don't think that.'

Amy went on to tell Harriet all that had happened right until the evening of a few days before when she had her fruitless conversation with her father.

'I know he loves you, Harriet, but he says he is too old and can't bear that you might reject him.

'But, Amy, he is not that much older than me.'

'That's exactly what I said but he won't take any notice of me, Harriet. I've got to say it whether you like it or not or if you think I am interfering. If you love Dad and you want him, you'll have to go and tell him and make him realise the truth. You are the only one who can tell him, Harriet.'

There was complete silence as Harriet digested these outspoken words. Then she turned to the silent girl by her side.

'Amy, you are right. It's up to me but how? I could if I had your courage. You might be younger but you are not afraid to say what you think is right.'

She kissed Amy's cheek.

'Thank you for coming to talk to me. You have given up your day with John to come here, haven't you?'

'No, I haven't given up anything,' Amy said with some spirit. 'I just want you and Dad to be happy. And, Harriet, I would like you for a step-mother as well as for a friend,' she added rather naughtily.

'Amy Holley, how dare you say such a thing! But I will take an example from you and I will try to talk to Daniel. I can't think of a way but if you can do it, then so can I.'

'Thank you, Harriet. That's the nicest thing I've heard for a long time. Well, I think we've left John long enough. Shall we go and look for him?'

Harriet looked slightly shocked.

'Does John know, too?' she asked.

'No, your secret is safe with me and I hope it won't be a secret too much longer.'

After Amy and John had gone, Harriet sat long and quietly. She had much to think of. She kept hearing Amy's words.

'If you love Daniel and you want him, you must go and tell him so.'

She did love Daniel. She did want him — for ever. But how to go and tell him? She sat until the darkness fell and she was tired but she was still no nearer to a solution to her problem. She lacked the confidence to face him.

She was still thinking about it by Wednesday and it was a visit to her friend, Lilian, which made up her mind for her. They saw each other regularly but Lilian did not know the story of Harriet's unhappy love until that day. Harriet set about to tell her friend of her problem and Lilian was a good listener and heard the story out.

When Harriet had finished speaking, she said bluntly, 'So there you are, Lilian, you know it all. Shall I go to Daniel as Amy says or not?'

'You go,' Lilian said, without hesitation. 'There are times when a

185

woman is stronger than a man and she has to have the courage to speak out. If you don't go, you will lose Daniel. You tell me, do you want to lose him?'

Harriet smiled at the forceful girl.

'No, of course you don't,' Lilian answered the question herself. 'So you know what to do. Today is Wednesday. Go on Saturday.'

'Lilian Frost, you are bullying me!'

'Harriet Bray, I am doing it for your own good and you came for my advice. Are you going to take it?'

'Yes, Lillian, I am, and I'm so glad I came to talk to you.'

And Harriet did go to Waterbridge that Saturday.

She set off after an early lunch and went straight to Rhodes Place. She was almost shaking. She had never been to the house before and to be going for the first time on such a mission filled her with dread. She knocked and knocked but there was no-one there. She went back to her motor-car close to tears.

Surely she had not agonised for a whole week and now come for nothing! She swung the handle of the car again, making up her mind as she did so that she would go and find Amy's shop and ask Amy if she knew where Daniel might be. Amy would help her.

She found the little shop easily and pushed the door open almost shyly. As she stepped inside, Amy came through the curtain from the work-room.

'Harriet, oh, Harriet! You've come.'

'Yes, I've come, but, Amy, what a beautiful shop. You have done well.'

'You haven't come here to talk about my shop. Have you seen Dad?'

'There's no-one at Rhodes Place, Amy. What shall I do? I could only think to come and ask you but I wanted to see the shop in any case.'

Amy looked at her watch.

'Nearly three o'clock,' she said. 'I'll tell you where you'll find Dad unless I'm very much mistaken. As regular as clockwork he goes for a walk along the river, across the fields where . . . '

She stopped, appalled by what she had almost said.

'Amy, my dear, you needn't worry that you will upset me. I know where you mean and I will go there, after I have a look round the shop.'

In the end, Amy had to push Harriet out of the shop but at last, the reluctant girl got into the car and drove through the town. She stopped by the river and started her walk across the fields in search of Daniel. With each step, she got more and more nervous.

There wasn't a soul in sight and certainly no sign of Daniel.

Amy must be mistaken, she thought. She walked steadily, forcing herself to keep up her pace. She passed the small wood, she passed the trees still vivid in her memory then she crossed another field. She was getting farther and farther from the town and had almost reached the railway bridge.

Did Daniel come as far as this? She was giving up hope but she knew that she could cross the bridge on foot and continue the walk on the other side, eventually going back into Waterbridge along the canal.

She was halfway across the field nearest to the bridge when she thought she saw him. She stopped, unsure. Someone who had been standing on the bridge, looking down into the water was now descending the steps into the field. She could see that it was a tall man.

She waited, not moving, her heart beating rapidly. He was walking towards her and, seconds later, she knew from the proud tilt of the head and the distinctive colour of his hair that it was Daniel. Harriet couldn't stop the cry that escaped from her, all thoughts of nervousness and not knowing what to say fleeing from her. She needed only one word.

'Daniel!'

He stopped. She could not see the expression on his face but the entire pose of his body was tense with expectation.

'Daniel, it's Harriet!'

They both started to run towards each other and as they met, it was with a desperate clinging as though they could never let each other go. At last, Daniel held her away from him and looked into her eyes.

'Harriet, my darling girl, what are you doing here? I was just thinking of you. I am always thinking of you.'

She was near to tears.

'I couldn't find you. I went to Rhodes Place, then I went to Amy's shop and she told me I might find you here. I left the car and started walking along the river but you were nowhere to be seen.'

He laid his cheek against hers.

'I am here now,' he said simply.

'Thank goodness,' she said. 'It was hard enough to come at all but all that is over. I have found you.'

He had to ask a direct question.

'Why did you come, Harriet?'

She looked at him, startled. She had not expected him to be so blunt and desperately she tried to explain.

'All these weeks, Daniel, I hoped you would come. I hoped for a letter even. But no word, nothing. I was so sure that you loved me but something told me that you were not finding it easy to get in touch with me. So I made up my mind that I would come to you. Have I done wrong?'

'How can you do wrong? To me you are perfect.'

'I am not, Daniel,' Harriet cried out. 'I am not.'

But he stopped her with another question.

'And what have you come all this way to say to me, Harriet?'

She looked at him. The fine, handsome face, the keen grey eyes, the bronzed lines of his face and those eyes returned her look searchingly.

'I love you,' she said fearlessly. 'I love you with all my heart and I want to be with you, for ever.'

The last words hung in the air between them for endless moments then once again Harriet found herself crushed against him. His strong arms bound her to him and his kiss loosened the fettered passion of the last months. Then it was Daniel's turn to speak.

'You dear, brave girl, to come to me. And here have I been, fearful that you would not want me. I did not dare put my love to the test. Can you possibly love a coward, Harriet?'

'I love you as you are, Daniel, and I can understand the difficult time you've been through. You had physical and emotional worries that I have never known.'

'I was afraid I was too old for you. I have a family nearly grown up.'

Harriet started to laugh.

'Daniel, I am not exactly a youngster. In any case, I love your family, and they will be my family, too.'

She had Daniel laughing with her.

'So you are going to come and live with me and my family, are you?'

She faltered only for a moment.

'Is that what you want, Daniel? Yes, of course I will.'

'Oh, Harriet, my dearest darling, I don't know why I am treating you so badly. Did you think I wasn't going to ask you to marry me?'

'I don't know.'

'Harriet, will you marry me? There, I've said it at last.'

'Yes, I will, Daniel, yes, please.'

They kissed again but he was still hesitating.

'But, Harriet, I must say it. I would marry you today, next week, but it is only three months since Dorrie died. I feel I must wait a while in respect to her. It is only proper. Can you understand, Harriet? Will you wait?'

She put her arms round him and her voice was soft.

'I would wait for ever, Daniel.'

Other titles in the
Linford Romance Library

SAVAGE PARADISE
Sheila Belshaw

For four years, Diana Hamilton had dreamed of returning to Luangwa Valley in Zambia. Now she was back — and, after a close encounter with a rhino — was receiving a lecture from a tall, khaki-clad man on the dangers of going into the bush alone!

PAST BETRAYALS
Giulia Gray

As soon as Jon realized that Julia had fallen in love with him, he broke off their relationship and returned to work in the Middle East. When Jon's best friend, Danny, proposed a marriage of friendship, Julia accepted. Then Jon returned and Julia discovered her love for him remained unchanged.

PRETTY MAIDS ALL IN A ROW
Rose Meadows

The six beautiful daughters of George III of England dreamt of handsome princes coming to claim them, but the King always found some excuse to reject proposals of marriage. This is the story of what befell the Princesses as they began to seek lovers at their father's court, leaving behind rumours of secret marriages and illegitimate children.

THE GOLDEN GIRL
Paula Lindsay

Sarah had everything — wealth, social background, great beauty and magnetic charm. Her heart was ruled by love and compassion for the less fortunate in life. Yet, when one man's happiness was at stake, she failed him — and herself.

A DREAM OF HER OWN
Barbara Best

A stranger gently kisses Sarah Danbury at her Betrothal Ball. Little does she realise that she is to meet this mysterious man again in very different circumstances.

HOSTAGE OF LOVE
Nara Lake

From the moment pretty Emma Tregear, the only child of a Van Diemen's Land magnate, met Philip Despard, she was desperately in love. Unfortunately, handsome Philip was a convict on parole.

THE ROAD TO BENDOUR
Joyce Eaglestone

Mary Mackenzie had lived a sheltered life on the family farm in Scotland. When she took a job in the city she was soon in a romantic maze from which only she could find the way out.

NEW BEGINNINGS
Ann Jennings

On the plane to his new job in a hospital in Turkey, Felix asked Harriet to put their engagement on hold, as Philippe Krir, the Director of Bodrum hospital, refused to hire 'attached' people. But, without an engagement ring, what possible excuse did Harriet have for holding Philippe at bay?

THE CAPTAIN'S LADY
Rachelle Edwards

1820: When Lianne Vernon becomes governess at Elswick Manor, she finds her young pupil is given to strange imaginings and that her employer, Captain Gideon Lang, is the most enigmatic man she has ever encountered. Soon Lianne begins to fear for her pupil's safety.

THE VAUGHAN PRIDE
Margaret Miles

As the new owner of Southwood Manor, Laura Vaughan discovers that she's even more poverty stricken than before. She also finds that her neighbour, the handsome Marius Kerr, is a little too close for comfort.

HONEY-POT
Mira Stables

Lovely, well-born, well-dowered, Russet Ingram drew all men to her. Yet here she was, a prisoner of the one man immune to her graces — accused of frivolously tampering with his young ward's romance!

DREAM OF LOVE
Helen McCabe

When there is a break-in at the art gallery she runs, Jade can't believe that Corin Bossinney is a trickster, or that she'd fallen for the oldest trick in the book . . .

FOR LOVE OF OLIVER
Diney Delancey

When Oliver Scott buys her family home, Carly retains the stable block from which she runs her riding school. But she soon discovers Oliver is not an easy neighbour to have. Then Carly is presented with a new challenge, one she must face for love of Oliver.

THE SECRET OF MONKS' HOUSE
Rachelle Edwards

Soon after her arrival at Monks' House, Lilith had been told that it was haunted by a monk, and she had laughed. Of greater interest was their neighbour, the mysterious Fabian Delamaye. Was he truly as debauched as rumour told, and what was the truth about his wife's death?

THE SPANISH HOUSE
Nancy John

Lynn couldn't help falling in love with the arrogant Brett Sackville. But Brett refused to believe that she felt nothing for his half-brother, Rafael. Lynn knew that the cruel game Brett made her play to protect Rafael's heart could end only by breaking hers.

PROUD SURGEON
Lynne Collins

Calder Savage, the new Senior Surgical Officer at St. Antony's Hospital, had really lived up to his name, venting a savage irony on anyone who fell foul of him. But when he gave Staff Nurse Honor Portland a lift home, she was surprised to find what an interesting man he was.

A PARTNER FOR PENNY
Pamela Forest

Penny had grown up with Christopher Lloyd and saw in him the older brother she'd never had. She was dismayed when he was arrogantly confident that she should not trust her new business colleague, Gerald Hart. She opposed Chris by setting out to win Gerald as a partner both in love and business.

SURGEON ASHORE
Ann Jennings

Luke Roderick, the new Consultant Surgeon for Accident and Emergency, couldn't understand why Staff Nurse Naomi Selbourne refused to apply for the vacant post of Sister. Naomi wasn't about to tell him that she moonlighted as a waitress in order to support her small nephew, Toby.

A MOONLIGHT MEETING
Peggy Gaddis

Megan seemed to have fallen under handsome Tom Fallon's spell, and she was no longer sure if she would be happy as Larry's wife. It was only in the aftermath of a terrible tragedy that she realized the true meaning of love.

THE STARLIT GARDEN
Patricia Hemstock

When interior designer Tansy Donaghue accepted a commission to restore Beechwood Manor in Devon, she was relieved to leave London and its memories of her broken romance with architect Robert Jarvis. But her dream of a peaceful break was shattered not only by Robert's unexpected visit, but also by the manipulative charms of the manor's owner, James Buchanan.